Lone Star Angel

by

Linda Carroll-Bradd

Lone Star Angel

Cover Art by *R.J.Morris*

The Wild Rose Press
PO Box 706
Adams Basin, NY 14410-0706
Visit us at www.thewildrosepress.com

Publishing History
First Cactus Rose Edition, December 2006

Published in the United States of America

Dedication

To my dad, Robert Carroll, who inspired my love of a good western story.

Chapter One

"Whoa, Star, just a little breeze. Nothing more." Carni Wendell pulled the reins to the left, wondering if she should have paid the stable master to drive her out to the Bar-T Ranch. This time she promised herself she wouldn't be a burden as a visiting relation, so she'd hired the horse and cart for the month.

In the distance, dark clouds chased the afternoon sun from the base of a craggy mountain. A chilly wind blew across the west Texas hard-packed prairie, twisting a dirt devil and tossing stray tumbleweeds across the path. Star stopped and nickered as an apparition appeared on the horizon.

A dark horse with a rider cantered in her direction and stopped not ten feet away, scraping up a dust cloud.

"Take a wrong turn, lady?"

The broad-shouldered man's voice was deep and full of suspicion.

"Easy, Star." With effort, she pulled the prancing horse back to an uneasy stand and turned her attention to the stranger. His hat shaded his eyes, but couldn't hide a strong jaw covered with beard stubble and a tight mouth pulled down at the edges.

A loose tendril of hair tickled her forehead. With a gloved hand, she tucked it under the knitted scarf wrapped over her ears and neck to fight off the chilly air. "I'm looking for the Bar-T Ranch. Would you know if I'm on the right lane? Can't really call this uneven, pot-holed path a road." She paused, expecting the silent stranger to answer.

Leather creaked at his shift in position. He rested a forearm across the pommel and stared.

"The stable master in Wayside Gap told me to turn south at the double fencepost. Not that I'm too good with directions, but those were the only double posts I saw."

"Thought I recognized Einhardt's mare."

What? The man commented on ownership of a horse, not about the boundaries for a cattle ranch? She waited for his confirmation she was headed in the right direction. "So, I did take the correct turn?"

"Could be." The man stood in the stirrups to peer over her shoulder. "What's your business here?"

Carni's gaze was pulled to the muscles straining the thighs of his muddy denims. The man obviously worked hard for a living. How dare a ranch hand question her? Rudeness was not to be tolerated. Grasping the reins with one hand, she reached under the cart seat to collect the velvet reticule lying at her feet. "I'm tired and I'm cold. As wonderful as our conversation has been, I need to get to the Bar-T ranch. I'll pay you four bits to direct me to the ranch house."

She dug out the coins and held them suspended over the side of the cart, staring with a narrowed gaze at the man's shadowed face. When he sat as still as a statute with only his eyes tracking her movements, her temper simmered. However, discussing her personal business with a ranch hand was unthinkable. She shook her hand and raised an eyebrow in his direction. "Okay, six bits." Another coin was added to her hand.

The wind teased her skirts, flipping back the hem to reveal several inches of a red petticoat.

His gaze flicked to the exposed lingerie and the right side of his mouth quirked for just a second.

She saw his reaction and steamed even more. He'd taken advantage of the wind's mischief instead of averting his gaze like a gentleman would. "A dollar for the directions. Take it now, I *won't* be offering more." Money well spent to remove herself from the belligerent company of this quiet man.

Several moments passed before he clucked out of the side of his mouth and urged the horse forward until abreast of the cart. "Whoa, Hades." He held a cupped hand under her outstretched one, looked up from under the brim of his black hat and winked.

Heat flashed through her at his bold gesture. With a quick movement, she released her hand and let the clinking coins drop into his gloved hand. "Your boss will be hearing about your surly attitude."

He shrugged and wheeled the horse, guiding it to the middle of the path. "Follow me." Without a look over his shoulder, he trotted up the small rise and disappeared over the top.

Carni sat staring at the fine figure he cut—shoulders straight, back erect, legs moving in perfect rhythm with the horse's stride. Then she shook herself out of her trance and snapped the reins against Star's back.

Just wait until she reached the ranch house and passed on this conversation to her sister, Amethyst.

Her horse trotted up the hill and started down the far side. The stranger was nowhere to be seen. Only a few puffs of dirt settling back to earth. Not thirty feet further was a lane leading to a grouping of buildings that must be the Bar-T.

To think her destination was almost in sight and that insufferable man had taken her money to lead her up a teeny-tiny hill. In agitation, Carni's fingers tightened and the horse stumbled.

"Oh, not you, Star. You're doing just fine."

Only a few minutes passed before she pulled the cart to a stop in front of the ranch house. In the open door of the barn stood two men. Even by squinting, she couldn't tell if one was the dark stranger she'd met on the trail.

The front door of the ranch house opened. "Carnelian?" A short, round woman dashed onto the porch, wiping her hands on an apron. "Is that really you?"

"Have I changed so much?" At the wistful note in her older sister Amethyst's voice, Carni battled guilt over her lengthy absence from family contact. That was in the past. "Didn't you get my wire?"

"A telegram? Oh, saints preserve us." The woman slapped a hand to her chest. "What's wrong with Momma? Or it is Poppa?"

"Nothing's wrong. They're fine—the last I heard. You always were such a worrier." Carni tied off the reins, grabbed a handful of her skirts and climbed down from the cart. "Aren't you happy to see me, Ame?"

Ame rushed down the steps and enveloped her in a tight embrace. "Of course, I am. I'm just surprised."

The scents of yeast and flour wafted into Carni's nose. She returned Ame's hug and allowed herself a moment of family connection. Raised in a loud and hectic household of eight children, Carni missed her siblings and enjoyed catching up with their lives. But on her own terms. "I did send you a wire. When was the mail checked in town?"

Ame straightened and held her at arms'

length. "Mr. Tarrant goes every week or so."

"Every week! Lordy, you're more isolated out here than I'd thought."

"Let me look at you. Five years is a long time. You're all grown up, but so thin." A wide smile crinkled the skin around her eyes. She ran her hand down the sleeve of Carni's outer coat. "Nice rich fabric. So, what did your wire say?"

Carni forced a smile and crossed her fingers for luck that she'd made this believable. "That I'd been missing you and was coming to spend the holidays on the Bar-T."

"Last letter from Mama said you were staying in Ft. Worth with Jasper."

Carni waved her hand and laughed. "Oh, I was. Until I learned he had business in St. Louis. I didn't want to take the chance that he wouldn't return in time. Besides, I wanted to see how you're doing in your new job and I haven't been to this part of Texas." Well, at least she didn't think she had. During her days with the Hegarty gang, they'd ridden over all parts of the Texas-Mexico border.

"Ame, I'm tired and parched. Could I have some tea?"

With both hands clasped to her chest, Ame shook her head. "Where are my manners? Of course, that is the perfect solution. We'll discuss your...visit...over hot tea." She linked an arm through Carni's elbow and led her up the porch steps. "You sit here a moment, and I'll call someone to take this horse to the barn."

"Thanks, but I'll stand." With a sigh of relief, Carni leaned a shoulder against a porch post. "My belongings will need to be unloaded first."

Ame grabbed the wooden sides and peeked over the edge of the cart, her eyes rounding at the cargo inside. "All these?"

"What do you mean by 'all'?" Carni brushed at the traveling dust that had accumulated on her jacket. "I brought only the bare essentials." Stiffness weighed her legs, muscles pulled from driving the cart, an act she hadn't gotten used to in the year since her life was shattered. A casual gaze around the yard revealed no one besides Ame. She slipped a hand around to the back of her skirts and squeezed her backside, rubbing at the aching muscles.

****

Luc Tarrant strode through his house, intent on discovering the identity of the stranger on his ranch. What the hell was some prissy city woman doing riding around in a flimsy cart when the sky was about to crack wide with a Texas thunderstorm? At the sound of his new housekeeper's voice, he slowed his steps.

The women chatted companionably, as if they were well acquainted. That didn't bode well for a man who demanded routine in his household. A muscle ticked in his jaw. He rounded the corner of the parlor and stopped at the sight through his front window.

On the front porch was the infuriating female that had treated him like a bellboy on the road, massaging her backside in the light of day.

In a flash, wild images ran through his head. Crazy thoughts of substituting his hand for hers. He shook away those unfamiliar ideas, pulled open the front door and stepped onto the porch. "Perhaps I can be of assistance?"

The red-haired stranger whirled. "You!" She raised a hand and pointed at his chest. "You owe me a dollar."

"Carni, what are you saying to—"

Luc raised a hand in his housekeeper's direction, not wanting his identity revealed just yet. Let the green-eyed city lady dig herself in deeper. "How do you figure that?"

She narrowed her gaze then turned to address the other woman. "On my way here I encountered this…" She looked over her shoulder, her gaze scanning his frame and focusing on his muddy boots. "This ranch hand."

From the corner of his eye, he saw Ame clamp a hand over her mouth, her wide-eyed gaze jumping between them.

With fisted hands planted on her hips, the redhead squared off opposite him. "I asked him if I was on the right path to this ranch. Instead of answering my question, he charged me for directions I didn't need."

"You offered." He shrugged and crossed his arms in front of his chest, enjoying this verbal sparring. "At the time, you seemed eager enough for them."

Her hands dropped to her sides. "If I'd known I was so close—"

"But you didn't. And I'm not opposed to earning an honest dollar."

"That's just it." She spun. "Ame, I want you to report this man to your boss. Tell him of my displeasure that his employee didn't have the courtesy to escort me safely to the ranch house. Why are you shaking your head?"

"I'm so sorry." Ame hurried up the stairs to stand by the new arrival.

The woman brushed dust off the front of her skirt. "Well, thank you."

With an exasperated sigh, Ame grabbed her arm and turned her. "I wasn't talking to you, Carni. I was talking to my boss. Mr. Luc, I'd like to present my younger sister, Carnelian Wendell. Carni, this is the owner of the ranch, Luc Tarrant."

At the word 'boss', the red-haired stranger jerked and turned, blacw hat bobbing with the movement. Green eyes widened and her rosy lips formed a moue.

Carnelian—unusual name. A likely description for the pretty city lady. Luc stepped forward and extended his hand. "A proper introduction?"

Carni looked at his hand then lifted her head and met his gaze. "I don't know what to say." With a slow movement, she slid her hand into his and shook. "I saw your work clothes..." Her cheeks heated and her gaze skittered to the side, "...then when you didn't answer..."

"Never mind that." For an instant, he savored the feel of her small hand nestled into his. Then he realized the wrong direction of his thoughts and forced grit into his voice. "Are you passing through? To El Paso, maybe?"

When she pulled away her hand, she cast a pleading look at her sister. "Ame, help me here."

Ame shook her head then turned to face him. "Mr. Luc, seems that Carni wired ahead about her intended visit." Her fingers fidgeted with the apron. "The telegram must still be in town."

The fidgeting was his first clue. "If it arrived at all."

Ame cleared her throat and squared her shoulders.

Another bad sign. Luc Tarrant didn't like the sound of what might be coming. Whatever it was, he'd face it like he did the rest of his life—straight on. "I'm listening."

A tight smile appeared on Ame's lips. "My sister's come to spend the holidays here on the Bar-T."

Chapter Two

Irritation clenched his jaw. So the woman wasn't just passing through. This meant changes to his routine. His carefully constructed routine. This sassy woman would be under his roof for the next ten days? Impossible.

Carni approached, her posture stiff. "Mr. Tarrant, I realize this situation is awkward." She tugged at the hem of her jacket, ran her hand down her front buttons then looked up. "I have been known to speak before I think. I can only plead irritation at not knowing the way and the tiredness from my journey."

Luc scanned her face and noticed tight lines around her eyes and a pinched look in her face, as if she'd recently lost weight. Up close, her eyes were banked with a sadness in their depths he hadn't noticed earlier. "My ranch is small and probably more rustic than a lady like you may be accustomed to."

"You'd be surprised the rustic places I've been." A short laugh escaped her lips. "I assure you, I'm happy for a roof over my head and the companionship of my sister at this special time of year."

Luc heard a note of desperation in her voice, but her gaze never wavered. Admirable. He glanced at Ame's concerned face. Where the hell did he fit this fancy lady into his household? A part of him admitted he'd be a heel if he sent the woman packing. He marched down the steps to the back of the cart, grabbed a couple valises and shot a look over his shoulder. "Ame, we'll clear a corner of the office for your sister."

"Yes, sir." Ame reached out and grabbed Carni's hand.

When he climbed the stairs, he spotted smiles on the women's faces. "Tell Rey to get the boys to hammer together a bed frame." He stopped beside them and narrowed his gaze on Carni's form. "How tall are you?"

She stiffened. "Why would you need to know that?"

"Lumber's precious. No need to waste any." He set down the valises and moved up next to her, intending to judge where her head came on his body.

Her eyes widened, but she stood her ground. "I believe the modiste said I'm five feet four."

He lifted a hand and held it above her head. The scent of lemons drifted from her body and he inhaled. Bad idea. "Tell Rey five and a half feet by two and a half feet. And he's to use the oldest calving ropes." He tucked one of the valises under his arm, grabbed the other by the handle and strode into the house. Over his shoulder, he said, "You ladies will have to come up with a mattress."

****

Ame whirled and grabbed Carni's hands. "You get to stay!"

Unwilling to display her immense relief, Carni raised her chin a notch. "Was there ever a question?"

Ame's grip squeezed. "Mr. Luc doesn't like changes here on the ranch. He has a routine and everyone keeps to that."

"Everything changes. Life sees to that." A fleeting thought of her horribly changed circumstances flashed through her mind. A fact she knew too well. Scratchiness hit the back of her eyes, and she blinked hard.

Luc strode back onto the porch and shot them a narrowed look.

Ame leaned forward, her violet gaze flicking to the cart and back. "I must tell Rey. Go, carry something inside. Mr. Luc demands work from everyone on the ranch."

"Demands?"

"Shh, just do it. Please, Carni." Her gaze pleaded, and her grip tightened before she scurried off the porch and stopped a moment next to Luc.

Carni couldn't hear her sister's words— probably offering profuse thanks. She supposed she could bring in a case or two. The thought of her special scrapbook sent her feet stepping lively across the wood planks and down to the cart.

Ame walked down the path toward the barn.

Carni stepped up to the cart. "I'm looking for—"

"Here, take this one." Luc had his hands on the round top case holding her toiletries.

"That's not the one I need. I'm looking for the square one with the leather corners."

With a huff of exasperation, he straightened and thumbed back his hat. "Miss Wendell, they all have to be unloaded. I'll pass them to you."

A shiver ran through her at the sound of her name spoken in his deep tones. Oh, oh. Not a welcome reaction. She looked around the dusty yard, hoping one of his "boys" would appear and relieve her of this unaccustomed task. "Okay, let me have it." She stretched her arm and grabbed at the handle, brushing the back of his hand, the bristly hair tickled her palm. A gasp escaped and she looked at him to see if he'd noticed.

Luc's amber eyes were focused on her face, brows drawn low. "Got it?"

She moved her hand further along the handle and hefted it. "Yes." She breathed deeply, fighting to get her emotions under control.

"Hey, boss," an accented voice called out. "What lumber did you mean?"

At the unfamiliar voice, Carni turned to see a wiry, tanned man striding toward them. Twenty feet behind him trailed her sister, whose gaze was glued to this man's back.

"Rey, help me with these. Then I'll show you

which lumber to use."

Carni picked up the case she'd just set on the ground and stepped out of the way.

The tanned man lifted his hat and dipped his chin in her direction. "Ma'am."

"Rey, I'm sure Ame told you this is her sister. Miss Wendell, my foreman, Rey Ignacio."

Again, the sound of her name coming from his mouth jangled her insides. Carni didn't know whether or not to put down her case for a proper introduction. "Hello, Mr. Ignacio."

"Around here, I'm called Rey." He stood next to the cart and raised his arms. "Here, boss, hand those down." He leaned over the side and scanned the back of the cart, his gaze widening then shooting to her.

For the first time, Carni realized the peculiarity of her appearance in this area of west Texas. A woman of obvious substance arriving at an isolated ranch. She gripped the handle tighter and turned toward the house. A fleeting thought went to the reason behind her flight to this place. Everyone needed to be somewhere. And all she wanted was a short chance to catch her breath and share remembrances of a happier past.

Ame bustled past and crossed into the house. "Come inside, Carni, and leave the way clear for the men. There'll be some...rearranging to do before we can get you settled."

Carni stepped into a homey, plain room with a rag rug on a plank floor, a pair of rockers angled toward a fireplace, a settee set against the window wall, and a steamer trunk served as a side table. All fabrics in the room were some shade of brown. The room screamed for a spot of color.

Footsteps shuffled on the plank floor behind her. "Excuse me, ma'am."

Carni moved onto the rug and watched as the men carried in her belongings, adding these to the ones Luc unloaded earlier. Within a short time, the stack at the edge of the room grew to a small mountain. She was aware of Ame standing to one side, mumbling and wringing her hands. "Is there a problem, Ame?"

"There're so many. I don't know about finding space."

"Don't worry. I always make do." She spread out her arms. "Why don't you give me a tour of the house?"

"A tour? There are only five rooms."

Surely, that wasn't the case. Didn't a man hire a housekeeper when there was a lot of work to be done? "I'd like to see them."

"All right, then I have to finish preparing supper. Oh, and get your tea." Ame waved a hand at the front room. "Here's the parlor, where we sit sometimes of an evening." She walked toward the back of the house. "There's the kitchen and this is where we serve the meals."

The scent of roasting meat hit her nose and Carni's stomach rumbled. Her meal at the depot in Waco had been hours ago. She surveyed the large room with a long table flanked by benches. On the stove, several pots steamed and bubbled.

"Let me check these before I show you the rest." Ame grabbed a towel and opened the oven, then lifted lids off pots and stirred the contents. She shot a glance at the clock on the far wall and winced.

Carni couldn't ignore the stab of jealousy at Ame's apparent ease in the kitchen. The array looked like when Sadie Mae had cooked for the whole family while they were growing up in Houston. All Carni had ever learned was how to cook breakfast. "Is there room for a kettle? Tell me where to find the fixings and I'll get the tea myself."

Ame turned with a smile. "Oh, Carni, that would be helpful. I've still got to shape the rolls." She jerked her head to the corner hutch. "Tea is on the top shelf in the metal tin."

"And the teapot?"

"Sorry, there's none. I pour water over a few leaves in the bottom of mugs."

She bet Ame hadn't shared that fact with Momma in the letters she was sure Ame wrote more regularly than she ever had. Every household of note had a full tea service. She removed her coat and hung it over the back of a chair, then gathered what she needed, noting every mug had chips on the edges.

While she waited for the water to heat, she walked the perimeter of the room, taking note of bins of potatoes, carrots, onions and various kitchen implements stored on shelves, recognizing only half of them. She came to a curtain hanging in a doorway. "Oh, is this the pantry? Will I find sugar?" She raised a hand to pull back the curtain.

"Not the pantry." Ame called out. "That's...my room."

The strident note in her sister's voice warned Carni too late. She'd already moved aside the rough blanket nailed to the lintel, displaying a narrow room containing only a bed and a chest of drawers. Two dresses and a coat hung from nails on the wall. The shock of the sparse furnishings made her pull the curtain closed, and she glanced over her shoulder. "I didn't mean to invade your privacy."

When she turned back to her tasks, bright spots of color dotted Ame's cheeks.

Carni put it off to being near the hot stove. The kettle whistled, and she busied herself with preparing the tea.

A bump and a scuffle sounded and the door burst open. She jumped and steaming water splashed onto her clothes. "Hand me a towel quick, Amethyst."

"Are you burned?" Ame rushed to her side and pressed a towel into her hands.

"No, I just spilled." Carni dabbed at her wet skirts, while shooting glares at the source of her surprise.

Luc entered, walking backward and

carrying one end of a rough wooden structure, Rey carried the other. "Set it here for now. First, we'll clear a space in the office."

Carni couldn't help but notice the way the broad muscles in Luc's back moved as he maneuvered the wooden structure criss-crossed with ropes against the wall.

The men moved down the short hallway and out of sight.

Slowly, Carni turned to her sister, realizing this was the second time today she'd stared after the owner of this ranch as he moved from her sight.

"Ame!" A masculine yell came from the back of the house.

Carni jumped. "Does he always bellow like that?"

"Coming, Mr. Luc." Ame's lips pressed tight before she turned and walked across the floor.

With a shrug, Carni sat at the table, blowing across the surface of her hot tea before tasting it. Bitterness assaulted her mouth and she wished for a spoon of sugar. She sighed. This time she would have to do without. Bumping and scraping sounded from the other side of the wall, and she was intrigued at what might be happening. She switched sides of the table so she could see down the hallway without being too obvious.

Ame came around the corner, carrying several books and stacked them on the floor in the far corner of the kitchen.

Rey followed with another armful and placed his stack next to Ame's, brushing an arm against her as he did. They exchanged a lingering glance before returning down the short hallway.

With a heartfelt pang, Carni watched the sweet exchange between her sister and this swarthy man. Looked like Ame had found someone special.

More bumping and muffled conversation. Once Luc emerged carrying a small trunk and disappeared into the room across the hall. A room she could only assume was his bedroom. A thrill ran through her. What personal items would he have in his sanctuary? A prized tintype? A remembrance from his youth? Did he have family?

Why would she care to know those facts about a stranger? Interesting.

Boots scuffling on the planks brought her attention back. When the men stepped into the hall, she looked up and met the direct gaze of his hazel eyes. Heat rose in her cheeks at the direction of her thoughts. Why she was even thinking along such familiar lines, she certainly didn't know. Must be fatigue brought on by travel.

The men struggled to fit the bed frame through the door, mumbling what she assumed were curses.

"Thank you again, sir." Ame returned to the kitchen.

The men strode through the room and left through the back door.

Carni refused to watch their departure. Instead, she glanced over her shoulder at her sister's hurried movements. "Come sit at the table to enjoy your tea, Ame."

"Oh, the tea. Thank you." Ame reached for her mug and, leaned a hip against the sideboard, before she took a sip. "Too much to do to sit."

"Surely, you can take five minutes."

"No, I have only an hour to get the meal on the table. I don't know how I'll get a ticking prepared by nightfall." Her gaze flicked around the room.

"Who else is helping you?" Amethyst's averted gaze bred guilt in Carni's conscience. She hadn't realized how her visit impacted her sister's workload. When she'd visited older brothers Malachite in Santa Fe and Jasper in Ft. Worth, the arrangements were complete, and she just moved into waiting rooms. "I'll help." She stood and extended her hands. "Here's another pair of hands. Give me a task."

"Do you cook now?" Ame's tone was hopeful.

Carni winced. "Not really, but I'm great at arrangements and decorating. Let me set the table."

"Well..." Ame set her mug on the sideboard. "The plates are usually stacked next to the stove, and I serve up the food as everyone passes."

"Everyone?" Carni eyed the long table. "How many are here?"

"Eight, uh, nine now that you're here."

"Okay, I'll set for nine." She walked to the hutch and opened a door. "Are the plates here?"

"In the lower cupboard."

The next half hour passed quickly while the sisters worked side by side. As she set out napkins and silverware, Carni tried not to bother Ame with too many questions. The poor woman never seemed to stop moving—checking the rolls, stirring pots, slicing meat.

Ame brushed the back of her hand against her forehead. "Now to fry the potatoes and we'll be ready."

"Let me try something different. Malachite's cook did this once and I watched."

"I'm not sure, Carni. Mr. Luc is particular about his food."

"Goodness, for one time the potatoes can be different." She rolled up her sleeves and grabbed the closest towel, tucking the ends into her skirt. "Point me to your kitchen tools and go back to your business."

With uncertainty covering her face, Ame pointed. "In the drawer of that bin table."

Carni grabbed a likely tool and set to work, pleased she'd figured out a way to contribute.

Chapter Three

Luc tossed his hat on the back porch bench and reached for the washbasin and towel. He spotted sawdust on his shirtsleeve and dusted it off. His thoughts went to the reason he'd been in the barn cutting lumber—the beautiful red-haired and green-eyed reason. The unexpected guest who he couldn't get off his mind, no matter how hard he tried.

His wood supply had been saved for making repairs to the back wall of the barn. But he'd make do. He always did.

Rey joined him. "Hand me the basin, and I'll pump the water."

"I'll do it." Caught woolgathering, Luc shouldered past him and yanked on the pump handle, grateful for the action to release his irritation. The basin filled, and he carried it to the bench.

"Not much of a resemblance between Ame and her sister." Rey moved closer. "One's blonde, the other's red-haired. Do you see one, boss?"

"A little." Luc felt his hands tighten before plunging them into the water. "Same shape to their faces, maybe." He splashed water on his face and ran wet hands over his hair, then grabbed the towel and moved to one side.

Rey stepped in front of the basin. "Pretty lady." He chuckled before he dipped his hands in the water.

"Watch yourself, Ignacio." Luc tossed the towel onto the bench and stomped into the kitchen. He'd worked hard today, and he was ready for a good meal. His steps slowed at the sight before him. His normally bare table was set with enough cutlery and crockery for an army—small plates, silverware, glasses and mugs. A jar of dried flowers sat in the middle surrounded by colorful gourds.

Where had Carnelian found those? He stilled. When the hell had he started thinking of the new arrival by her first name?

He bristled at the excess and opened his mouth to remind Ame about his guidelines.

From behind came the sound of male conversation by several of his hands.

Rey moved into sight. "Dios mio."

Carni stepped forward and, with a sweep of her hand, indicated the table. "Gentlemen, take a seat. You'll be served at the table tonight."

"Move aside." Izarra scurried into the room, hands tucking pins into the bun at the back of her head. "Ame, sorry. Why you didn't call for me?"

Luc reached out a hand and rested it on his old housekeeper's shoulder. "Because we keep telling you, Izarra, this is your time to rest."

With a grin, she slapped at his hand and tsked under her breath before moving deeper into the room. "Plenty of time when I die. Now, what I can—" She stopped and glanced over her shoulder at Luc. "Who's this?" She broke into her native Spanish, shaking a finger in Luc's direction.

Ame stepped forward and linked arms with her sister. "Mrs. Jacinto, this is my sister, Carnelian, come for a visit."

"Ah, que bonita." The older woman grasped Carni's hands and squeezed.

At the sound of scuffling feet behind him, Luc moved into the room then walked to the head of the table. "English, please, Izarra."

The next few minutes were loud with benches scraping and quick introductions around the table. Ame and Carni dished up and delivered the filled plates to the table. All waited for them to be seated.

Luc leaned toward Ame. "Where's the potatoes?

Her gaze shot between her sister and back to him. She chewed at her lower lip. "Not ready yet, sir."

He leaned his chair back so he could see the stove. No frying pan in sight. "I don't understand. Where's the pan?"

"I'm sorry—" Ame gulped.

"Don't apologize for my actions, Ame. I'll explain." Carni turned to him, a bright smile on her lips. "Tonight we're having pommes duchesse. They're in the oven for a few more minutes."

Silence followed her words and the others exchanged glances.

Clamping his jaw tight so he wouldn't be rude to the guest, Luc grabbed his fork and stared at his thick slice of roast. At least, he still had gravy.

"Were the storm clouds I saw on my drive from town really heading this way?"

From the corner of his eye, Luc saw Carni lean forward and look down the table at the others. He wondered who would be the one to tell her meals were normally quiet events.

Rey leaned forward, looking around Matro next to him. "Nah, wind scared them north. No rain tonight, maybe none tomorrow."

"But plenty cold tonight." Izarra made a show of rubbing her arms and shivering.

Luc reached for his coffee cup. His empty cup. He tipped it toward Ame and raised a questioning eyebrow.

Her gaze went to the full glass of water at his place. "Coffee'll be ready with dessert."

"Drinking water with meals is better." With a nod, Carni gazed around the table. "I learned that from a chef in Denver, or maybe it was San Francisco. He told me the bitterness of coffee masks the flavors of the food you're eating. Water lets you enjoy each and every taste."

Another change. "What I'd like to be tasting are my potatoes."

"Oh! The potatoes." Carni stood and dashed into the kitchen. The oven door clattered and a shriek sounded.

"What the hell?" Luc bolted from his chair and into the kitchen.

Carni stood with her hand plunged into the water pail and wisps of smoke curled from inside the oven.

Not promising for the potatoes. The pang in his chest at her pained expression stopped him dead in the middle of the floor.

"What happened?" Ame rushed in and grabbed her sister's arm. "Are you all right?"

"Just a little burn. But the pommes duchesse are a tad brown."

Ame grabbed a towel and pulled out the pan, using her body to shield the view. "Mr. Luc, we'll be right back. Give us a moment, please."

One last gaze at the room and he returned to the table, his boots dragging at the unexpected response to Carni's injury. He sat and grabbed his glass of water, chugging half.

All looked at him, obviously waiting for an explanation.

"Minor mishap, that's all."

"But the potatoes—"

"Stow it, Juan. Wait and see."

Luc grabbed a roll and smeared it with butter, wondering how his household had spun out of control in only a few hours. His office in an upheaval, lumber conscripted to make a bed that would be used for only a few days, and now the contents of his regular Saturday night dinner disrupted.

The women returned to the room—Carni with a scrap of cloth wrapped around her left palm, Ame with a pan of brown pyramids which she quickly served onto everyone's plates.

Suspicious looks passed between his employees.

He jabbed a fork into the strange shape and sliced off a piece, almost afraid to taste hard potatoes. Another sacrifice to placate this city woman.

****

An hour later, Luc rubbed fingers across tired eyes and rolled his shoulders against the cramp of sitting hunched over the ranch ledgers. He tossed down the stub of a pencil. No matter which way he added the figures, they came up short of his goal. Oh, they'd have plenty to eat and the money in the bank would cover emergencies.

Just no extras. No building the second story to the house or the extra section to the barn.

Laughter erupted from the dining room. From the volume of the sound, no one had headed their way when they'd finished their pie, like he had. Carni's stories of traveling along the Texas-Mexico border reminded him too much of his upbringing and he'd excused himself to come in here. Now he stood and moved toward the half-closed door, eager for a distraction from his disappointing discovery.

Carni's voice rose above the others adding one last line to her story and laughter burst again.

He leaned a foot flat on the wall and tilted his head back until he met resistance, then closed his eyes. The buzz of conversation was enjoyable from this distance—close enough to know people were near, but not close enough to be expected to share events from his past. He strained his ears for the sound of her confident tones.

"Oh, excuse me."

His head snapped around, and he looked into surprised green eyes. The scent of lemons teased his nose.

She held up the coffeepot. "You've been in here so long I thought you might want a refill."

"Sounds good." He stepped to the desk and grabbed his mug, extending it. "I'm about finished here anyway."

The metal lip clinked against the crockery as she poured. "I don't want to rush you. Today's been long and I need to unpack a few things before getting settled for the night."

Up this close, he spotted flecks of gold in the lady's eyes. The mother lode. What a strange thought. For a distraction, he sipped at the coffee and scanned the room. His gaze landed on the empty bed frame. "There's no mattress."

She set down the coffeepot on a stack of papers on the desk. "I know, not enough time today. But tomorrow's another day. I told Ame I didn't mind sleeping on the settee."

Luc set down his cup and rubbed a hand over the stubble on his chin. By rights and as host, he should offer her his bed, but that seemed too personal. And he'd never fit on that small sofa. "Least I can do is help you get settled."

"That's not necessary." She stepped forward with a hand outstretched. "I don't want to put you out any more than I have already."

The papers slid and the coffeepot tipped, dribbling dark liquid down the spout and puddling on top of his open account book.

"Damn." He jumped toward the desk and grabbed up the ledger, tilting the book over the wastebasket so the coffee ran off.

"Oh, I'm sorry. Let me get a towel." Worry wrinkled her brow as she turned toward the door.

He reached out a hand and touched her shoulder. "No need, it'll dry." The shoulder under his hand stiffened for just a moment then relaxed, as if she'd made a decision about him. A momentary impulse to caress her jolted him, and he dropped away his hand. "Tell me which cases you need in here and I'll bring them."

After transporting all her cases into his office, he said goodnight and moved to the kitchen, hearing the door close behind him. All he wanted was a few moments of breathing the crisp night air to clear his senses of her lemony scent.

Ame jumped up from the table when he entered. "Mr. Luc, I can't thank you enough for allowing Carni to stay. My sister's been—"

He rested his hands on the back of a nearby chair. "Ame, no more thanks."

"All right." Her shoulders drooped then she shook herself. "Sir, I'm working on setting up for breakfast and the coffee pot is missing."

An excuse. This was his reason for seeing the intriguing woman one more time. "I know right where it is. I'll get it." He turned on his heel, walked down the hallway and rapped on the door to his office.

"Yes?" Carni's voice sounded muffled.

He cracked open the door a couple inches, suddenly aware of what her muffled tone might mean. "Ame needs the coffee pot."

"Come in. It's still on the desk."

With a push, he stepped into his office. Or what, up until five minutes ago had been his office. Now it looked like back stage at a theater on opening night. Every one of her cases gaped open, displaying an assortment of clothes and personal items. Dresses of quality fabric were tossed on every available piece of furniture. Petticoats of bright red, deep purple, vivid yellow. Thin night rails with tucks and lace.

The cost of what he saw before him would probably keep this ranch running for six months. Irritation at the extravagance burned in his chest, and he turned to her.

She stood with a book of some type pressed

to her chest, eyes wide and glassy.

But all he noticed was glorious wavy hair spilling over her shoulders and halfway down her back. Red shiny hair that caught the flickering lamplight and glowed like embers. Poetry, from him? Only with restraint did he keep from crossing the room and running his hands through her hair to see if it was as warm as it looked. "Sorry to disturb you."

Ironic were his choice of words. As he moved to the desk to retrieve the metal pot, he realized 'disturbed' exactly described how he felt.

And all because of this woman.

Chapter Four

The next morning, Luc sat on the edge of his bed and tugged on his boots, weary from a night of restless sleep. The image of Carni in the midst of those riches preyed on his mind. Why did a woman of obvious wealth need to stay at a poor ranch? Until the day before, Ame had barely spoken of her family.

As he stepped into the hallway and walked toward the back of the house, he outlined what he wanted to tell the hands at the morning meal. The thoughts fled his mind when he spied the beauty stretched on his settee.

She lay on her back with one arm thrown over her eyes, one slim, pale arm. Wavy red hair flowed across one shoulder and hung over the edge of the furniture.

He stopped at the edge of the rug and stared, his chest tightening. Why was he affected by this stranger, this rich stranger? They had nothing in common and from the sounds of her lifestyle, she'd be flitting off on another adventure as soon as the holidays ended.

Enough! He spun on his heel and followed

his nose to the smells coming from the stove. The ranch hands sat around the table, sipping coffee. He lowered himself into the chair at the head of the table and nodded when Ame delivered his plate. "Morning."

Heads rose, eyes blinked in his direction and a couple mumbling voices answered him.

Ten minutes later, the men filed out of the kitchen ahead of him, drawing on jackets, gloves and hats as they moved. He paused with a hand on the door, wondering how to politely word his request. "Ame?"

She looked up from where she stacked empty plates, light eyes wary. "Yes, sir?"

"Find some other task for your sister today. Don't let her cook my potatoes." Content his routine would be as he liked when he returned, he crossed the back porch and headed across the dirt yard, ready to start his day.

****

A shaft of sunlight crossed her face and Carni scrunched shut her eyes. When she rolled to her side, muscles pulling along her back told her she'd been in one position too long. She groaned and leaned up on one elbow, listening for movement in the rest of the house.

If she were truthful, she'd admit she was listening for the rumble of Luc's deep voice. Too early in the morning for the truth. All she heard were pots banging in the kitchen. Her sister was obviously at work. A glance at the clock told her she'd slept through the morning meal. Guilt settled over her and she swung her legs over the edge of the settee. Sleeping late was not the sign of a good houseguest.

Within minutes, she'd tossed on her plainest dress, pinned up her hair, visited the necessary and reentered the kitchen. "Sorry for sleeping in."

Ame turned from the tub filled with sudsy water. "You must have been tired to sleep through the noise of the morning meal. I kept a plate for you in the warmer."

"Thanks." Carni busied herself with pouring coffee and finding silverware. Instead of going to the table, she set the plate at the end of the counter. "We've barely had a chance to talk. So, tell me how you ended up here, in this part of Texas."

Ame's gaze narrowed. "What does that mean?"

With a fork of eggs halfway to her mouth, she paused. "Ame, I'm making conversation. When I left home..." Her thoughts touched on the impetuous act that turned her life down a path from which she was still recovering. "Last time I saw you—"

"I was in my bed, and you were climbing out our bedroom window with a laugh and a wave." Ame sighed and turned back to the dishes.

She knew she deserved her sister's tart words, but the statement still stung. "I was going to say you were studying music and being courted by that peculiar head clerk in Poppa's shipping company. What was his name?"

Ame's shoulders slumped. "Horace Wimbleton."

"Oh, yes, we used to call him 'horrible Horace'." She giggled. "Does he still work for Poppa?"

Ame winced and looked down. "No, he died last year. Consumption. A horrible way to die."

The tone in her sister's voice warned Carni to stop right there, but she plunged on. "How on earth would you know that?"

"I nursed him." Her voice dropped to a whisper. "He was my husband."

"Oh, Ame. I'm sorry, I didn't know." She rushed around the end of the counter and threw an arm around her sister's shoulders. "Jasper didn't say a word."

Ame straightened and lifted her chin. "You should know our brother doesn't gossip. Besides, my year of mourning passed a while ago."

Carni thought of her own loss of how Jordan had been taken from her. Was this the perfect time to share her own loss and tell Ame the truth about her life? The need to tell burned in her mouth.

Izarra burst into the room, arms full of dried flowers. "Morning, ladies. Aren't these pretty? I'm adding to the vase. I like what Miss Carni did last night."

The moment was gone. Carni wondered if the time was ever right to reveal one's sordid past. To share the worries and regret she'd carried over the past few years.

She pasted a smile on her face and turned to the older woman. "Those are lovely, Izarra. They must have been beautiful when they were fresh." Thinking about her mistakes wouldn't fix them. She had to find something else, something happier to think about.

Dabbing butter on her last bite of biscuit, she popped it into her mouth and gazed around her surroundings. "This place needs color."

Ame glanced at the plate on the counter and then up. "You want to paint?"

"Not paint." Carni waved a hand in the air. "Decorate. Christmas is in less than a week, but I don't see any sparkle in this house."

With a shake of her head, Ame turned back to the dishes. "I wasn't here last year. I don't know what is usual."

Carni glanced over her shoulder at the woman humming while she slid dried stems into the jar on the table. "Izarra, does Mr. Luc have decorations to put out for Christmas?"

When the woman turned, her expression was cloudy. "I say to him always, you must put out a star at this special time of year." She shook her head and raised her hands, palms up. "But he say, no time for that and not to waste money."

Carni tapped a finger on her chin as she thought. "So he didn't say no to decorations." She turned and leaned her hands on the counter. "Remember Momma's tree, Ame? With the silk ribbons and the glass balls. I used to love helping her make the house look pretty."

"I remember." She looked over her shoulder. "And putting it all up was such fun. The boys stringing the garland from the eaves and on the staircase. And Sadie Mae's baking." Ame's eyes took on a dreamy quality. "The tangy scent of her gingerbread cookies filled the house for days."

"Let's do that."

"Do what?" Her brows lowered.

Carni spread her arms wide to indicate the house. "Make a Christmas like that."

"Impossible."

"I know it can't be exactly the same, but we could bake cookies and decorate them."

"*We* could bake?"

Carni laughed. "Well, you could bake, I'll decorate. There's nothing to use as garland, but there must be a way to spruce up the place."

Ame's face darkened and she shook her head. "We can't spend any of Mr. Luc's money."

"We don't have to. I can go into that little town—"

"Not a trip to Wayside Gap. Carni, no one is free to take you."

Carni fisted her hands on her hips, irritation stiffening her backbone. Ame seemed determined to deny her scheme. "Why would someone have to take me? I drove myself yesterday."

"Women don't travel by themselves. Too

dangerous—Indian attacks." Ame swiped at the pan in the sink. "Tell her, Izarra."

"Si, es verdad." The older woman's graying head bobbed. "Oh, yes, is true. Only Mr. Luc rides alone to town."

She shrugged off their warnings. "Well, I didn't know, and nothing happened." Had she really been in danger on her drive? Other than from the tall man who'd refused to help her with directions. She shoved that thought to the back of her mind.

"Besides, we have to be practical." Ame turned and leaned her hip on the counter, her lips pressed into a straight line. "We need to sew a mattress cover and stuff it for your bed."

"I hate practical. I'd rather make holiday decorations." A thought went to the way her back had ached upon wakening, and she dismissed it. One more night on that settee wouldn't be too bad. "That's more fun."

Ame laughed and shook her head. "Well, that hasn't changed about your personality."

Carni made a face at her sister and turned to Izarra. "Do you have any holiday decorations?"

"One year, Matro make me a big star out of barbed wire. We set on front porch."

Carni clapped her hands. "That's a great start. Maybe we can get him to make a couple more."

"Carni, Izzara and Matro have their own house down by the bunkhouse. The star decorates their porch."

"Oh, of course." Carni pressed her lips together—another instance of speaking before thinking.

"We bring to big house. I want Mr. Luc's house to be pretty." She moved to where Ame stood drying her hands and grabbed them. "This year, we put decoration to Mr. Luc's house, and he will like them."

Carni liked the older woman, liked that the woman knew fun and laughter were necessary. "Let's think of other items."

"Well, Momma always had shiny things to make the house pretty. Foil cards and pierced tin stars on the fireplace mantel."

"Shiny, huh?" Carni thought of the multitude of silk dresses in the next room. One thing she was good at was sewing. The newspaper accounts of Jordan's raids on the stagecoaches always mentioned his fine suit of clothes. "I have just the thing." She marched into the office and surveyed the choices. Not the cranberry silk suit, that was her favorite. She filled her arms and returned to the long table in the dining room. "Here, let's use these."

Ame gasped and stepped to the table, an outstretched hand caressing the fabrics. "Carni, such beautiful dresses. We can't tear these up."

"These old things? I can always buy more."

"You can?" Ame's eyes rounded. "Ones like these?"

"Sure, once I get back to a big city."

Enthusiasm for this project bubbled inside her. "I want to use these to decorate."

"Okay, but..." Ame's fingers lingered over a skirt of green linsey-woolsey, her gaze wistful.

Carni peered at the worn cloth of her sister's work clothes and remembered she'd seen only two other dresses hanging from hooks in Ame's small room.

"Ame, do you want this?" She inched the garment closer. "Maybe we could let it...I'm sorry."

"Why? I'm definitely rounder than you." She looked up and smiled. "If you're willing to donate these, I'm game to help with decorations. Let me get my sewing basket."

****

By mid-afternoon, the sisters had ripped apart two skirts, making strips they sewed together in a long garland chain. Bright red and yellow silk petticoats were cut into thin ribbons. Wanting to keep the decorations a surprise, they'd stashed everything in Ame's room when the men came inside for the noon meal. Unable to suppress their enthusiasm, the women had shared secret glances around the table. The men were too busy talking about the ranch work yet to be done that day to notice.

Once the men left and the meal dishes were cleared, Izarra brought the star inside.

Flanked by the other women, Carni stared at the crude five-pointed star shaped from barbed wire. "This star needs to go up high.

41

With ribbons of bright silk streaming from its points." She glanced around the house but didn't see the right place. "I know, on the roof.

"The roof?" Ame grabbed her sister's arm. "Oh, Carni, I don't know about that."

"The location is perfect." Carni set her jaw and nodded her head. "I won't consider another."

The women laughed as they worked, sewing silky decorations with lace to hang from doorknobs and making multi-colored silk chains to drape on the window sill. Carni felt more at home than she had in a long time. How had she thought living in hotels would be satisfying?

Ame stood, resting a hand on her hip. "I need to stop now and finish the last things with supper."

Carni looked at the disarray of thread, fabric and lace scraps, and the pile of decorations. She rolled her shoulders at the pleasant ache caused by doing something useful. A feeling she'd missed. "We have done well, ladies. Izarra, you should pick out a few to take to your house."

"Oh, can I, Miss Carni?" She smiled wide and her dark eyes flashed with pleasure. "These will make mi casa shine."

"Carni, that angel you made is wonderful. You have a talent for sewing and such detail on her gown. "

At the unexpected praise, heat flooded Carni's cheeks. Jordan had always taken the decorative touches she added to his clothes for granted. "She's not done yet. I want to add buttons or pearls."

"Too bad we don't have a tree like Momma's. You could put her on the top."

"I'm thinking of putting it on the mantel."

"That'll be a great place." Ame turned.

Carni reached out and grasped her sister's hand, fighting the sudden tightness in her throat. "Ame, you don't know what being here means to me. I know I didn't give you much choice—what with the wire going astray."

Ame blinked quickly and squeezed her hand. "I'm glad, too. But neither of us will be if the meal is late."

Carni released her grip and watched Ame hurry off to the kitchen. She ran a finger over the stuffed head of the cloth angel in her hands. Something was needed for the hair. She'd find that later. Now she wanted to put up some of these decorations for all to enjoy.

Gathering up the long chain of their "garland", she wandered into the parlor and eyed likely spots. But the chain was too long for this room. Maybe outside. She dashed to her room for her coat and then stepped onto the front porch.

Within minutes, she'd walked off the distance of the porch roof and done a rough measurement of the fabric chain. Draping the edge of the roof would work with a bit extra on each end. Rather than bother Ame with a request for hammer and nails, Carni figured she could tie the cloth in place.

After a quick look around the area to make sure she was alone, Carni dragged a chair over to the edge of the porch and stepped up on the railing. One arm hugged the post and she balanced both feet on the rail. With a one-armed throw, she tossed the tied bundle onto the roof and clambered up behind it.

When she straightened, she took a moment to catch her breath and inched sideways to the peak of the roof. From up here she had a clear view of the layout of the ranch. The barn, the bunkhouse, Izarra's small house, the corral with several horses. Past the barn was the larger corral where she spotted several men working with cattle.

Only a moment of concentration passed before she spotted Luc's tall figure moving among the men and animals with a confident stride. Even at this distance, he cut a handsome figure.

A chilly wind ruffled her hair, and she shivered. One glance at the sky filled with low, gray clouds told her she'd better hurry. Moving back to the edge of the roof, she sat and untied the ends of the chain. Next she tossed each end toward opposite sides of the roof and stretched the chain across the shingles.

The front door opened and footsteps rang against the wooden planking. "Carni, don't tell me you're on the roof!"

"I'm stringing the garland chain."

Ame's blond head appeared in her line of vision. "Oh, do be careful."

"Stop fretting. You can tell me if the swags are even."

She'd knotted the fabric at the top of one post and let a length hang below the roof edge, tucking a folded edge under a shingle. A gust of wind blew again and her foot slipped, dropping her to her rear. "Oh."

"Carni, maybe you should come down."

She scrambled to her hands and knees, tugging her skirts from under her feet. "I want to finish this." She moved to the next section and tucked in an edge. "How does that look?"

"Fine." Ame hitched her shawl tighter around her shoulders. "Feels like snow tonight."

Carni's hands burned from the cold and her fingers fumbled to move the fabric into the small space under the wood.

"That one's a bit long. Can you pull it up?"

She forced a grin to her stiff lips and rearranged the strip. "Okay, how's that?"

"Great. Carni, I have to get back inside. Hurry before you freeze."

She raised her hands to her mouth and blew on stiff fingers. Only a couple more swags. The wind gusted, pulling the fabric over the edge of the roof. She lay flat to pull it up and the wind tossed her skirts over her back, cold air running over her pantelet-covered legs.

"Blast and darn." She moved quickly to set the last two swags then reached over the edge to tie off the end. But she reached too far and swung over the edge of the porch, legs kicking and skirts flying.

"What in hell are you doing?" Luc's disapproving rumble sounded.

Carni glanced over her shoulder at Luc standing by the back of the house where he'd obviously come from the direction of the barn. He stood with legs braced apart and arms folded over his chest. The brim of his hat shadowed his eyes, but she'd bet they weren't smiling.

"Stringing garland for holiday decorations." Her cold hands ached from their grip on the rough wood. "Could you help me?"

He stood still.

"I'm not going to pay you."

"Ask nicely, Miss Wendell."

She eyed the distance to the ground, wondering how far the drop was, but worried about spraining an ankle. Then she'd be no help to her sister. "Help me, please?"

He covered the distance in several long strides and reached for her ankle.

The moment his hand closed around her ankle, Carni had second thoughts. Did he expect her to let go and then his hand would travel up her leg to her hip? Under her skirts. And...

"Maybe that won't work." He released his grip. "Just let go and I'll catch you."

She glanced over her shoulder to him standing directly below her with arms outstretched. She had to trust him. "Don't drop me." She loosened her grip.

"Don't slide your hands."

"Ouch." Too late. The pain of a splinter stabbed her hand before she let go and fell. To land within the cocoon of his strong arms. The urge to nestle her head against his chest hit hard. How long since she'd felt a man's embrace, felt safe?

At that thought, she turned her head to look into his eyes. His hazel gaze slowly rose from staring at her mouth.

Uh oh. She knew that look. One that her own gaze probably mirrored.

His eyes flared, and he muttered, "Ah, hell." Right before his mouth descended and his lips brushed against hers, at first soft. Then his hold tightened, and his lips pressed harder, drawing out her response.

She squirmed around until she could wind her arms around his neck and answer his kiss with one of her own. The passion built and threatened to burst into flame.

Luc stilled and loosened his hold, letting her legs drop free. "Ah, Miss Wendell, that—"

Carni struggled to open her eyes from the effects of his kiss. She didn't like the closed expression she saw on his face. "Don't say a word. Unless you're going to tell me how wonderful that kiss felt." She braced her hands on his arms and landed on the ground, then stepped back. "After this, you should call me Carni."

Chapter Five

Although he knew he shouldn't, he couldn't tear his gaze away from Carni's figure as she moved around the front of the house and climbed onto the porch. Just before she entered the house, she turned to look at him and smiled.

His blood, already heated from that kiss, pumped faster through his body, circling low in his groin. A feeling he hadn't enjoyed in way too long. And shouldn't feel toward a woman who wouldn't be within arm's reach next month. The lemony scent from her skin still clung to his clothes. He sucked in a deep breath of cold air, telling himself to bring his body back under control. But knowing he wanted to maintain the connection to Miss Carnelian Wendell.

With measured steps, he followed the track she'd taken, pausing for several moments to look at the swag of green cloth drooping from his porch roof. Today was December 22nd. Only three days until Christmas. He'd been so focused on the ranch work, he hadn't thought ahead to the actual holiday.

If the weather held, he'd drive into town for supplies and pick up something for each of the hands. A token of appreciation for their hard work. A bit of something special beyond their salaries. If only he knew what might be best. Maybe he'd get Ame to write up a list of what to buy.

The wind blew, and his ears smarted from the cold. He was a fool to stand outside late on a wintery afternoon and stare at some foolish decoration. Better to be inside where he wouldn't be reminded of the reason for that infuriating woman to be hanging from the roof and having to drop into his waiting arms.

He stomped up the stairs and into the parlor, shucking his coat and hat onto the hall tree next to the front door. The movements caused lemon to rise to his nose and he inhaled. A noise sounded and he turned his head, caught by the woman whose scent he savored.

Carni stood at the fireplace mantel, arranging bright strips of cloth over the aged wood. "The ladies and I thought the house needed a bit of holiday cheer."

"The *ladies* did?"

"Well, I did make the suggestion." She squared her shoulders and faced him, her features drawn tight. "But don't worry. All of this," she waved a hand to indicate the room and then above her head, "and that, came from my trunks."

He gazed at her determined expression. His thoughts returned to the previous night and the sight of her in his office, red hair rippling down her back. Of this morning's view of her sleeping, her wavy hair in disarray over the pillow and her gown.

With an effort, he forced his thoughts back to safer territory. Back to his office that had been strewn with dresses and petticoats of every color. Her dresses, her petticoats, her under—. Breaking eye contact with Carni, he looked around the normally plain parlor. Bright colors that now dotted the room around him. Small pockets hanging from juts of limestone rock in the fireplace. Ribbons wove trails over the mantel. Streamers draped from the curtain rod.

Growing up with only a papa meant he'd done without homey touches for most of his life. Only vague memories remained of a light-haired woman who'd died when he was six. His memories were of sunshine and picnics outdoors—none of winter holidays or of Christmas traditions.

Hell, what did he know about geegaws and flouncy things? "I'm glad to hear none of this came from my supplies."

****

By rote movements, Carni set out the napkins and silverware for the evening meal, irritation building inside at Luc's rebuff of her efforts. Maybe she'd expected too much. In remembering her childhood, Momma was always the driving force for decorating the house at the holidays. Poppa had completed the tasks she gave him, but never with much enthusiasm.

What he'd loved was the singing. A grin came to her mouth at the memory of Poppa's strong alto providing the foundation to the rest of their voices as they gathered around Momma at the pianoforte. Oh, how she missed hearing her favorite carols.

"Carni? What's wrong?" Ame stood by her side. "You look sad."

"Just remembering Poppa singing Christmas carols." Carni turned and offered a wan smile. "I hadn't realized how much I've missed that until just now."

"Those were good times." Ame bumped Carni's arm. "Right now, we need to feed these hungry men. Help me serve the stew?"

Carni followed Ame toward the stove, wondering why she'd never been aware before of how much work was involved with keeping people fed. Had she truly not paid attention?

The meal passed quickly. Carni secured a place at the other end of the table, knowing if Luc made another comment about her impulsive decorating, she'd spout with a statement that could end her visit. A couple times, she looked up to see him frowning in her direction. Honestly, she couldn't think of another thing she'd done to cause those looks.

Finally, the coffee and apple cobbler had been served and the men tromped out, headed for a poker game in the bunkhouse. Suited her fine. As she stacked plates, she noticed the men's were scraped almost clean. Her sister was a good cook and had a receptive audience for her offerings.

Ame had found her role in life. Judging by the looks Carnie'd seen between Rey and Ame, they shared special feelings and Ame would be married again soon.

A twinge of jealousy pricked her chest. Carni wished she could find a new path for her own life. She shook away those thoughts and carried the plates into the kitchen. "Let me dry tonight, and we can get back to our decorations."

Ame smiled. "Thanks. I can always use the help."

"Wiping dishes is something I can do right." Her thoughts went to the attempt to decorate the house for the holidays and didn't know why Luc would be bothered by their efforts. The least he could have said was thank you. Did she dare ask and expose the fact she cared about his good opinion?

Best not to dwell on that. "Tell me, what do you think I should use for my angel's hair?"

Hours later, Carni sat curled on the end of the settee, her feet tucked up under her night rail. Using sharp scissors, she cut stitches holding decorative golden thread on the bodice of a jacket. The shiny threads would serve well as strands of hair on the mantel angel. Carni glanced at the stuffed doll that was quickly becoming special. She'd already stitched on closed eyes with eyelashes and a bow mouth.

The hair would be the finishing touch

The back door rattled and she heard the thud of heavy boot steps against plank flooring. Her hand stilled, she dropped the jacket over the angel and peered into the darkness past the circle of light cast by the oil lamp.

Luc appeared at the edge of the room and leaned a hand against the wall. "You're still 'wake"

His words were slow. She sniffed at the scent of whisky and tobacco floating into the room. "Just doing some sewing. Good card game?"

"Nah, I lost." He moved toward the fireplace and reached for fireplace screen. "Temperature's dropping. Need to build up the fire."

She watched his sure movements as he slid the screen to the side, jabbed at the glowing logs to stir up the embers, and placed a large log toward the back of the opening. She almost laughed at the thought he'd stirred her embers as well and now she didn't know what to do with those feelings.

He straightened, but still faced the fireplace. "Taking a trip into Wayside Gap tomorrow. Be the last one before Christmas."

At his words, she sat up. A chance to be of more help. "I want to go with you."

He shot her a frowning look over his shoulder. "Bound to be cold."

"I have a coat and gloves." She stood and gathered the blanket around her shoulders.

"There are things I want to contribute to the holiday meal."

"If you need anything, tell your sister to put it on the list." His gaze touched on her bare feet then rose to her eyes.

A couple steps took her to his side, but she restrained herself from reaching out to touch him. "Can't do that. I don't know what's available in the mercantile."

"Probably less than you're used to."

She stiffened, the impact of his words made her pause. Why had he returned to this gruff, distant attitude? "Are you saying I can't accompany you?"

"I'll make better time without you."

She shrugged. "Then I'll drive the rented cart."

He turned to face her, brows drawn down in disapproval. "Coming out here alone was a foolish act. I aim to have words with Einhardt about that."

She hated being called foolish. Her hands fisted at her sides, letting the blanket droop open. "Why? The man was just earning an honest dollar." The moment the taunt left her mouth, she regretted it, but refused to let her feelings show.

He gripped her shoulders. "I'll not be responsible for a guest of mine wandering around lost on the prairie."

She looked into his eyes to gauge if he'd drunk enough for the whisky to affect his actions. She'd lived through that once and wouldn't again.

Ever.

Looking up, she saw clear hazel eyes that held no meanness. "I know the way now and won't get lost on this trip."

His hands loosened to caress her shoulders and draw her inches closer. "Getting lost isn't the only danger."

The concern his words expressed went straight to her heart, but she couldn't put too much emphasis on what he said. What if he didn't mean any more than he would for any guest? "In broad daylight? I'll be perfectly safe."

"Has no one told you about the Comanche raids? I won't put your safety at risk." His grip tightened, and he pulled her into his embrace. "Not when I've just found you." His lips closed over hers, and his tongue pushed her lips apart then swept inside her mouth with bold strokes.

She grabbed his muscled back and clung, her mind swirling with his change in behavior and the headiness of his kiss.

His hands rose to her hair, and he pulled out the pins, letting them drop to the rug. Once the bulk was free, he ran his fingers through the strands, and then bunched it up at the base of her neck. "As silky as I thought."

With her forehead pressed to his chest, she breathed deep, trying to catch her balance. Her heart pounded, and her breasts tingled at being smashed against his front. Aware of only a few layers of cloth separating their bare skin.

Gentle kisses rimmed her forehead. "Carni, we've got to stop."

Her skin tingled where his beard scraped. "Really?" She swallowed hard then nodded. "Yes, really."

He cleared his throat and stepped back, a hand rubbing the back of his neck. "Sorry, I—"

"I told you before not to apologize."

"Right." He leaned over to pick the blanket off the floor and wrapped it around her shoulders, tucking it under her chin. "Sure you'll be warm enough?"

She rubbed her cheek against the back of his hand. "I have no doubt. Now."

"Night, Carni." He leaned close and kissed her forehead then he moved away.

She closed her eyes and savored the warmth of his lips on her skin then turned toward the sound of his movements. "Luc?"

"Yeah?" He stopped at the hallway and looked over his shoulder.

"Tomorrow morning, don't leave without me."

****

Luc hunched his shoulders and scooted forward on the wagon seat, trying to use his body to shield Carni from the sudden wind. Another half mile to go. He didn't think she'd stopped talking for more than a few minutes during the hour-long drive.

"Ooo, that's chilly." She bounced on the

wagon seat, making the springs squeak. "Do you think we'll get snow for Christmas? I always wanted snow when I was growing up, but Houston is too close to the coast."

Part of him wanted to learn all about her. The other part cautioned practicality. "Storm's brewing." Luc squinted up at the gray clouds that had darkened and hovered lower over the past hour. "Can't say if it'll hang on that long."

With gloved hands, she pulled the edges of her coat tighter over her knees. "How much farther until we reach town?"

He glanced sideways, noting her smile as she gazed around. The cold air had reddened her cheeks and the tip of her nose. Only a deluded fool would mistake a shared ride to town for a desire for closeness. "Uncomfortable?"

With a wide smile, she turned toward him. "Just looking forward to getting into town. I love shopping and want to buy something special for Ame." She gave him at sideways glance. "For several at the ranch. Don't you love Christmas? I do. Oh, and birthdays. I used to look forward to my special day for weeks. Making all sorts of lists of what I wanted."

Uncomfortable with her line of conversation, he looked away. "Different than my childhood. If your birthday didn't fall on a Sunday, then you worked, same as the other days."

"Really? Oh, that's sad."

Was that pity in her voice? He stiffened. No need to relate any other details of his poor upbringing on the Texas-Mexican border. Several minutes passed with only the soft whistle of the wind to break the silence. The outlying buildings of Wayside Gap came into view. "Almost there."

She leaned forward. "Good, I'm ready to stretch my legs."

He guided the horses past the stables and called out to the blacksmith standing in the open doorway. "Morning, Gunther."

"Ah, gutten morgen. Building to good storm." His blacksmith apron flapped in the growing breeze.

"Temperature's dropping."

The man's words of response were whisked away.

Luc glanced down the main street, spotted billowing sheets on Mrs. MacQuaid's line and looked toward the rise at the far end of town. The clouds weren't far above the spinning weather vane on top of the church's bell tower. With clucks of encouragement, he guided the horses in the alley alongside the mercantile and tied off the reins.

For a couple moments, he debated about telling Carni his concerns about the worsening weather, but something held him back. Let her enjoy her shopping. "Remember, I have chores waiting back at the ranch. You may have to be quicker than you're used to."

Carni's eyes widened before she forced a smile. "I can try." She gathered a handful of her skirts and turned toward the far side.

He climbed down and came around the wagon, ducking his chin tight to his chest. "Give me your hand." He steadied her while she climbed down then guided her to the mercantile's door with a hand at her lower back. A slip of a thing like her could get swept up by the wind and tossed down the street like a stray tumbleweed.

Carni stumbled, and her hand shot out to the side. "Oops."

"I've got you." Luc grabbed her elbow with one hand and twisted the doorknob with the other. They burst into the store, laughing.

"Morning, Luc. Setting to blow out there?"

He released Carni's arm and shoved the door closed. "You're right about that, Karl."

Luc watched as Carni moved toward the bolts of fabric at the back of the store then walked to the scarred wooden counter and set down a slip of paper. "Here's what I need."

The storekeeper took the list and scanned it. "Got it all except the rope. Is the wagon on the side as usual?"

Luc saw Carni pick up several items and inspect them. He remembered her comment about gifts for those at the ranch. "Have any whisky in stock?"

"Always."

"Good. I'll take a couple, no, make that four bottles. The hands have earned their own treat." He glanced at the items in the Reinhard's display case, items he'd always thought were too expensive. "How much for the Swiss chocolates?" He winced when Karl stated the price. "Give me three boxes. And wrap those in brown paper."

Karl's gaze went to the back of the store and a grin touched his mouth. "Sure enough, Luc. Getting ready for the holiday?"

"You could say that." He leaned a hip on the counter and watched Carni examine lengths of fabric, holding them out then draping them across her skirt. "Might want to call in your wife to help. I know for a fact the lady intends to buy." He tilted his head toward the back. "When she decides, add her items to my total."

Karl's eyes widened, but he didn't speak. "Excuse me." Only a few steps were needed for him to reach the door leading to the living quarters. "Trudee, customer for you."

Luc strode to the window and peered outside, concern mounting at the darkening clouds. Across the street, a loose shutter on the Lucky Thistle Saloon flapped in the wind, resounding with a hollow thud. The owner, Broc Matheson, probably wasn't getting much sleep upstairs with that racket.

"Morning, Mr. Tarrant." Mrs. Reinhard closed the door with a click.

He looked over his shoulder and lifted his fingers to the brim of his hat. "Morning, ma'am."

"Stage brought the mail yesterday. A wire arrived for your new housekeeper." She turned to the shelf over the desk and grabbed a stack of envelopes, flipping through the pieces. "The one with the unusual name. And another for—"

"So I heard." Luc's gaze met Carni's across the store and they shared a smile.

"Trudee?" Karl stood in the doorway to the storeroom, a sack slung over his shoulder. "I believe the young lady needs assistance."

"Who?" She turned to her husband then looked around the store before moving toward Carni. "Oh, good morning, miss. My name is Mrs. Reinhard. What may I show you?"

As Luc turned his attention back to the worsening weather outside, the women's voices faded. They needed to leave...and soon. With the way the clouds were gathering, they'd be lucky to reach the ranch before the storm broke. He pivoted and strode toward the back of the store. "Karl, I'll help load the supplies. Car—, uh, Miss Wendell, you have about five minutes more then we're leaving."

The wide-eyed look she gave him over her shoulder was filled with dismay. "Oh Luc, I need more time to decide."

He speared her with a stare. "Storm's coming fast. Five minutes." Once he spotted her reluctant nod, he slid past the curtain and grabbed a sack of flour from where Karl stacked the ranch's supplies. On a nearby shelf, he spotted woolen blankets and tossed a couple on the stack. No use taking any chances.

When he returned to the store, Carni stood,

chatting with Mrs. Reinhard. A small pile of wrapped bundles sat on the counter between them. "I'll load these and come back to settle the bill."

"No need." The thin woman shook her head and gave him a big smile. "It's been paid. And then some."

Confusion stilled his movements. "What?"

Carni turned with an impish grin and rested her hand on his arm. "I insist, Luc. Since I'm obviously no help in the kitchen, I want to compensate you for my stay as a houseguest."

Fighting to ignore the pressure of her hand on his arm, Luc thought of the supplies in the wagon. Food stuffs that couldn't be used during her short visit. Ranch supplies that had nothing to do with this city-bred woman. He lifted his hat in the direction of the shopkeeper. "Thank you, Mrs. Reinhard." He scooped the pile of bundles into his arms and connected with Carni's gaze. "We'll discuss this later. I'll bring the wagon around front. Watch for me."

Two minutes later, Luc pulled the horses to a stop and set the brake. The wind had picked up and the first snowflakes floated down. He grabbed the porch pole and swung down to the boardwalk in front of the mercantile. Before he reached the door, Carni burst through and scurried to where he stood.

"I'm ready. Let's go." She cast a glance over her shoulder then looked at him, worry drawing her mouth tight.

He handed her up into the wagon and followed her, adjusting one of the blankets over her lap. While reaching for the reins, he glanced toward the mercantile, wondering what caused Carni's reaction.

At the window stood Sheriff Buck Taylor.

Chapter Six

Her throat tight with worry, Carni scooted close to Luc, ducking her head to rest against his shoulder. "Drive, please. Fast."

Luc released the brake and slapped the reins. "Get on up, Concho and Blanco." The wagon jerked forward and the horses moved in a tight turn to the right.

In this position, she hoped to keep her face out of the sheriff's sight. Maybe the lawman's gaze sharpened at the sight of all strangers to Wayside Gap, but his interest had felt personal.

Why couldn't she have stayed on the ranch? The decision to come to town had been impulsive and foolish. And, if she admitted the fact, a bit selfish. She'd wanted Luc all to herself for just a little while. With that thought, she tilted her head so she could watch his face for a reaction.

Luc turned and looked down, his gaze narrowed. "You okay?"

"Sure, just a little cold." The lie tasted like ashes in her mouth. "You don't mind, do you?"

"Nope. Maybe just what's needed to stay warm." He turned back to the task of urging the horses faster.

"Especially my nose." Carni snuggled her face deeper into Luc's shoulder until she was sure they'd ridden past the store. She was grateful for the new woolen scarf covering her ears and neck, the one Mrs. Reinhard had encouraged her to buy. Maybe enough of her head was covered so the sheriff hadn't noticed her red hair.

Scattered snowflakes danced on the breeze then drifted to the ground.

"Damn." Luc ground out the curse. "Under the bench is another blanket. Spread it over our heads and shoulders to keep off the snow. Gonna get colder."

Maneuvering while the wagon still rolled was tough, but she finally got them shielded. "Only a little snow. We can withstand it. And it's so pretty." The flakes fell faster now, and she stuck out her tongue to catch some.

Conversation proved difficult—Luc concentrated on driving the team and Carni's thoughts turned over plans for which sibling she'd visit next. Rather than bring trouble to Luc's ranch, she'd leave. Even if she didn't want to.

He snapped the reins, clicking his tongue at the horses. "We'll never make the ranch at this pace. Hold on."

As the wagon picked up speed, she wedged her arm around his and leaned close, her other hand gripping the edge of the blanket. Within minutes, she'd tired of watching the increasing snowfall and cold seeped into her boots and up her legs, making them ache.

The wind kicked up, blowing snow into their faces. The horses tossed their heads and whinnied.

Luc talked in a soothing voice and eased back on the reins, slowing them from a canter to a trot. Gusts blew the snow sideways and scooped up ground snow, dancing it across the path.

A horse stumbled and the wagon jolted sideways.

Carni screamed and gripped the bench, the blanket flapping against her side.

Luc struggled to steer the horses back onto the path and held them at a walk. "That was bad. Damn Diablo winds."

Fear tickled her stomach. She'd never been out in a winter storm and couldn't imagine how he could see to drive the team. "Maybe if we go real slow."

"Can't go much slower than a walk." He looked around, squinting against the driving snow. "Should be coming up on the double posts. From there, the eastern boundary of the Bar-T isn't far. We'll hole up in a line shack while this blows over."

The horses lowered their heads and trudged forward. Carni huddled under the blanket, wriggling her toes inside her boots to keep the blood moving. Her world narrowed to the solid warmth created by Luc next to her on the wagon seat, the backs of the pair of horses and the swirling flakes that surrounded them. Her thoughts drifted.

"There're the posts." Luc guided the plodding horses off the lane onto the trail leading to his ranch.

Carni roused and looked over her shoulder at the dim gray outlines in a blanket of white. "I can barely see them."

"Here, take these. I can't spot where to cut overland to reach the shack from up here." Luc passed off the reins to her and jumped down to the snow-covered ground. He leaned over the edge of the wagon and tucked his half of the blanket around her feet. His concerned gaze met hers. "You okay to drive?"

The minute he started fussing with the blanket, her heart warmed. She looked into his concerned gaze and nodded. "I can drive." Her gaze ran over the features of a handsome face that had become dear in such a short time. His ears were already red and his jaw clenched hard against the cold. She transferred the reins to one hand then unwound her new scarf. "Use this to cover your neck. I've got the blanket."

"Thanks." He took the scarf, wrapped it around his neck and pulled it over his mouth. As he inhaled deeply, his gaze held hers then turned and plowed through snow that came halfway up his calves. At the head of the team, he grabbed the halter of the bay horse and tugged it forward.

How long they took to get to the shack, Carni didn't know. She was too busy juggling the reins and fighting to keep the blanket over her head and shoulders.

Luc approached the side of the wagon, his hat dusted white with snow. "Hold the horses a bit longer, all right?"

"I will." She nodded, flexing her stiff hands in turn.

"I'll unload the supplies first then settle the horses in the lean-to."

Ten minutes later, Carni kneeled in front of a stone fireplace and fed twigs onto a puny fire. Behind her the door opened, letting in a gust of cold wind. The flame flickered low. "Oh, I'm no good at this."

"That's a start." Luc squatted next to her, dumping an armload of wood pieces. "Let me take over." He rearranged the burning wood and added more until light and heat radiated in their faces.

After warming her hands, she stood and spread out the blankets over the foot posts of the bunk bed and a table to let them dry.

Luc hung his coat on a hook by the door and pulled the chairs near the fire. "Getting warm?" He tugged off a boot.

"Yes, thanks." Her gaze went to his stocking foot. The intimacy of the situation hit her and her thoughts wandered.

"Might want to get out of your wet boots."

She sat and struggled with the sodden laces. Once the damp leather was off her feet, her toes instantly warmed.

With both stockinged feet pointed toward the fire, he leaned the chair onto its back legs. "Care to explain why you ran out of the mercantile?"

So he had noticed. She should have realized nothing slipped past this man. "You'd been clear about the need to hurry. I didn't want you to wait. That's all."

"Carni..."

The tone of his voice left her no choice. "The sheriff was looking at me too closely. Gave me the willies."

"So the sheriff stared. Why should that bother you unless you are on the run?" He laughed and turned his attention to the fire, jabbing at a log with the iron poker.

She bit her lip. "Not on the run...exactly."

With slow movements, he set down the poker and leaned his elbows on his thighs. "Carni, you've either broken the law or you haven't."

Carni jumped to her feet and paced the small open space. "What if a person didn't know what she was getting into? Does that count?"

"How could you not know? The law's the law." He leaned back again, this time with his arms crossed over his chest. "Did you break it?"

"Did I? No." Carni stopped behind her chair and gripped the wooden back. "Was I with those who did?" She sucked in a deep breath, knowing this would change his opinion of her. "Yes."

The chair crashed forward, and he stood. "How?"

The single word resounded through the small room. Carni wished she could touch him, but his expression was blank, unapproachable. "But I didn't know right away."

Luc jammed a hand through his hair and stalked to the back wall. He leaned a shoulder against the wall and stared. Waiting.

"I was young, only sixteen and so ready to be in love. A handsome, well-dressed man courted me away from my father's house." She glanced at Luc then stared at the fire while she relayed the rest of her sordid history. "He took me to concerts and plays and the finest restaurants in Houston. Just the way he dressed was more impressive than the clerk in my father's shipping company who kept being invited to our Sunday dinner table."

She paused, waiting for a comment from Luc.

None came.

"So when Jordan asked, I ran away from home with him. He promised we'd be married, but some detail kept preventing that from happening." Of all her revelations, this was the hardest. "After awhile, that didn't matter."

"What do your antics from several years ago have to do with the sheriff?"

Carni turned and faced Luc. "The man's

name was Jordan Hegarty."

Luc shoved off the wall, his body rigid. "Of the Hegarty stagecoach-robbing gang?"

She nodded. "By the time I learned that's how he earned his money, I'd fallen in love and couldn't leave."

Now he paced the room, taking only three strides before turning. "You go on any of the raids?

"No, I stayed back in whatever hotel was nearby." She lowered herself to the chair, mostly to clear a path for his agitated movements. "Toward the end, I hated what Jordan did. Even if he only hit payroll stages of big companies, the danger was always there. The last few runs, he worried the lawmen were getting closer."

Luc stopped across from her, hands on hips. "I read the stagecoach passengers were uncooperative in providing details. Never understood that."

Carni allowed herself a small smile. "That was due to one of my ideas. He never approached the passengers with a gun drawn and he always shared part of the take with them. That's where he got his nickname—The Gentleman Bandit. And the fact he wore the latest styles, that was my role. I kept the gang looking natty." She looked away, her throat suddenly dry. "Until the last time, when he didn't come back."

"Killed?"

"Gunned down." She swallowed hard. "Only

one came back, and he ran off to Mexico."

"Back to the mercantile." Luc grabbed the chair and turned it around, then straddled it. "Did Sheriff Taylor approach you? Speak to you?"

"No, but he sure stared." Her insides crawled at the memory of that narrowed gaze. "Maybe he thinks I know who the inside man was."

Luc chuckled. "Well, Carni, you are an attractive woman."

She flashed him a grateful smile. "Thank you, but Jordan protected me from knowing too many of the details. Said I couldn't keep a secret to save my soul." She gripped her hands in her lap. "But I did. All those years, I never told anyone, not even my family. I heard something about him having contacts at telegraph stations but—" She broke off and shook her head.

Across the few feet that separated them, Luc's gaze was intense. "If you did nothing wrong, don't be thinking of running."

"I can't help myself." She blinked hard at the burning behind her eyes. "If I'd been stronger, I would have left the minute I learned about the robberies. But I had nowhere to go.

"Why not back to your family?"

"At the time, I didn't think I could look Momma and Poppa in the eyes." She let out a big sigh. "Since visiting with my brothers and now Ame, I see that is a possibility.

For a long moment, she watched his face,

looking for an indication of what he felt. The uncertainty had her nerves jangled to a frazzle, and then a shiver engulfed her body. "I'm cold. I've got to dry these wet clothes."

Luc stood and walked to the window. "Snow's still falling, but sounds like the wind has died some. Drying our clothes is a good idea." He grabbed the blanket from the table and stretched it across a corner of the shack. One end was tied around the bedpost, the other hooked over the window latch. "There's a bit of privacy."

Carni ducked behind the makeshift dressing area, grateful for even the thin blanket between them. For just a second, she covered her face with her hands to collect her thoughts. He now knew the worst about her and hadn't acted repulsed. Maybe he would still let her spend the holidays at the Bar-T.

With fumbling fingers, she unbuttoned her skirt and untied the ribbons on her petticoats, letting them fall to the floor. While pulling her arms from the sleeves of her blouse, she snagged her fingers on the blanket and it dropped. She gasped and raised her arms to cover her chest. "Oh."

Squatting in front of the fire, Luc looked over a bare shoulder, his gaze running up her underwear-clad body.

Carni couldn't stop staring at his back, rippling with muscles. Broad shoulders that tapered down to a taut waist.

With controlled moves, he rose and turned to face her. "Stop looking at me like that, Carni."

"Like what?" She rubbed her hands on her arms, no longer certain the shivers were all from the wintery air.

"Like I'm lemonade on a hot summer's day. If you don't, I can't guarantee what will happen."

His chest was well defined with broad planes of hard muscle covered with tufts of brownish-red curly hair. She stepped over the pile of wet clothes. "Oh, Luc, I can't help myself. You look so strong and healthy. I need that right now." She closed the distance between them by half and then stopped less than two feet away.

"Change your mind?"

A tentative hand reached toward his chest, then dropped back to her side. "I have to know you want this, too."

"Almost since you offered to pay me for directions." With one long stride, he was before her and ran a hand from her elbow to her shoulder and around her neck, fingers teasing the length of hair that tumbled from her hairpins. "But I can want you and still not act. You're on your way somewhere else, Carni. I see it in your eyes."

"Everyone is going somewhere."

"Not everyone." He shook his head, his gaze intense. "Not me, I'm home. I grew up being hauled around by a vagabond father, chasing mustangs between Mexico and south Texas. Early on, I decided to save money and buy my own land. On this ranch is where I'll be until the day I drop from the saddle."

She let out a long sigh. "You have a purpose, a meaning to your life. I want that." Unable to resist, she ran a hand over his chest, delighting in the friction of coarse hairs covering warm, firm skin. "And I want this. The hard planes of your body pressed next to mine." She eased forward, placing a kiss on his stomach, then ran a line of kisses up his breastbone, her hand anchored on his taut waist.

His grip on her neck tightened and he sucked in a breath before whispering her name.

Stretching on tiptoes, she kissed a path upwards and nuzzled his neck. He smelled of leather and wood smoke and male musk. Scents she would always connect to Luc Tarrant.

Strong arms pulled her close, and his lips descended until they hovered only a breath away from hers. "You sure?"

She glanced up into his heated amber gaze and knew. If all they ever had were this one night, she'd never regret the experience. With the tip of her tongue, she outlined her lips, watching as his gaze dipped to follow the slow action. Then she leaned close enough to trace his lower lip. The movement brushed her breasts against his chest and she savored the tingle that swirled all the way to her feminine core.

He pulled her tight, and his lips covered hers.

The roughness of his beard rubbed her chin, arousing another part of her skin. She wrapped her arms around his waist and let her hands explore the hard bulges of his back.

Strong hands cupped her jaw, thumbs running across her cheeks. His tongue pressed her lips for entrance.

With a sigh, she opened her lips, welcoming his invasion. Everywhere their bodies touched, his warmth seeped into her.

His hand dropped to her shoulder, a finger caressing her skin under the strap of her chemise.

Her breasts felt full, aching to be touched.

Using a fingertip, he traced the lace along the neckline until he reached the ribbon tie. Then he broke the kiss and leaned back. "Carni."

The deep rasp of his voice curled her toes, and she struggled to open her eyes. "Yes?"

"Last chance. Once I see your naked skin, stopping will be harder."

Shifting her weight, she pressed her stomach against his front and felt the hard ridge of his desire. "This is plenty hard as it is."

One more long and measuring look then he scooped her up and carried her to the bunk bed against the wall. He unbuttoned his jeans and shoved them and his flannel drawers to the floor. Grabbing a blanket from where it hung, he climbed in next to her.

Carni snuggled close, sighing when she fit herself next to him. Too long since she'd felt like a woman, a woman who was desired by a good man. For only a moment her conscience niggled with questions about Luc and how her reputation could cause him harm. Then his hand was on her breast, and she forgot about anything, but the excitement between a man and a woman in this carnal pleasure that had spanned the ages.

Chapter Seven

The instant Carni woke, she knew the day would not go as she'd hoped in those hazy moments before sleep descended the previous night. She was alone in the bed. She stretched out a hand to touch the bunk where he'd lain. Cold—as if Luc had been gone for a while. Struggling to the edge of the mattress, she buttoned her chemise and scanned the room for the rest of her clothes. They were stretched across every available surface in the shack. Fire licked with orange and yellow flames around a small log to fight the morning chill.

She shivered anyway. Whether from the cold or Luc's absence, she didn't know. With shaking fingers, she pulled on her clothes and shoved her feet into stiff boots. A peek out the window confirmed a solid layer of snow covered the ground, but none fell from the sky. Instead, she saw a steady drip of snow melting off the roof. Grabbing her coat, she jammed her arms into the sleeves and stepped out the door.

Luc was about twenty feet away at the lean-to, brushing the bay horse. Snow mounded a foot high around their feet.

For just a moment, she let her gaze travel his strong figure, remembering how his body had felt next to hers. Carni needed to pretend she wasn't affected by his absence in the bed they'd shared. Last night she'd thought she'd be happy for just this one memory.

She'd lied. After last night, she wanted more. But she wouldn't cling. "Morning, Luc."

He glanced over his shoulder, his expression blank. "You're awake, good. I can heat some beans, or if you can wait an hour, we'll eat at the ranch."

Her heart chilled at his impersonal tone without a single word of greeting. Obviously, he was anxious to get back to the Bar-T. She flipped her hair over her shoulder, wishing she had her hairbrush. "I can wait. I'll be ready to leave in five minutes." Before she made a plea for them to talk about last night, she walked around the side of the shack until the structure blocked Luc from her sight and tended to personal matters.

Back inside the shack, she tidied the bedcovers and searched the floor for her hairpins. Not really caring about her appearance, she pinned back just the front of her hair to keep it from her face but left the rest loose. What else should be expected from someone who'd had to take shelter in a ramshackle building in the middle of a snowstorm?

The door opened, and he crossed to the

fireplace. "Wagon's outside." With the iron poker, he stabbed at the smoldering log and scattered the embers. "Do you have everything?"

"Yes, I do." Including her pride. She spun and marched out of the shack, dumped the folded blankets into the back of the wagon and struggled into the seat.

The door latched, and Luc cleared his throat. "Snow's deep. I'll lead the horses until we get onto the lane."

She edged to the middle of the seat and untied the reins. With a hand resting on the brake handle, she turned and looked down, careful to school her features into a helpful expression. "I'm ready when you are."

Problem was, she meant she was ready to discuss their wonderful night together. And Luc was waiting to hear she was ready to head out for the ranch.

For several moments, his gaze searched her face then he straightened and strode to the horses' heads.

Weak sunlight filtered through high, wispy clouds. From all around, Carni heard a symphony of drips—snow melted off the shack and lean-to roofs, bushes and shrubs. This snow wouldn't last another day on the ground. No white Christmas for 1868. She released the brake and leaned forward, the reins held loosely in her hands. This could be a long ride—in more ways than one.

"Let's go, Concho and Blanco." Luc's voice

held command and the horses responded, straining to set the wagon in motion.

Wagon boards creaked, harnesses jangled, and the iron-rimmed wheels crunched paths through the snow. Time passed in a blur. Carni's eyes ached from the glare of the sunlight on the expanse of white. The horses picked their way over the slushy snow and the slippery rocks underneath, Luc's soothing voice encouraging them forward.

Soon the horses turned left into the lane, and Carni looked up, spotting the ranch house with the barbed wire star on its roof, the barn and Matro and Izarra's small house. A sense of homecoming filled her, and she sat upright. Why had that thought crossed her mind? She didn't fit in here.

She didn't fit in anywhere.

During the drive, she'd figured out Luc's reason for keeping his distance. Her past. A good man like him wouldn't want an association with a woman having a questionable past.

The wagon pulled up and stopped in front of the porch. A repeat of her arrival only three days earlier.

Ame burst through the front door, dashing to the top of the steps. "Oh thank the stars, you're safe. I pictured you lost and wandering the prairie."

With sure movements, Carni set the brake and laughed. "On my own, that's where I would have been." Her gaze went to the tall man crooning to the horses. "But Luc knows his way."

"The storm was bad here with high winds." Ame descended the steps, her hands twisting the hem of the apron. "I hoped you might have stayed in town."

"Already on the road when the storm hit." Luc walked around to the back and grabbed an armful of supplies. "Ame, I'll be ready for bacon and eggs in ten minutes. And lots of coffee."

Carni shot a glance at Ame and saw her expression tighten at Luc's terse words. She wished he wouldn't take out his mood on others. If he was upset with her, he should tell her. She'd welcome an argument, or even yelling, over this ominous silence.

"Do you need help carrying anything?"

"And give you a chance to discover what your gift is?" Carni smiled, relaying her appreciation for the offer. "No thanks. But, Ame, that coffee sure sounds good."

With tired moves, Carni climbed down and leaned over the edge of the wagon, locating the paper-wrapped packages that were her purchases. She entered the house and paused for a long look at the familiar walls, a smile touching her lips at the small signs of holiday decoration. Surprising how special these four walls had become in such a short time.

Her gaze landed on her cloth angel. How sweet of Ame to have placed it on the fireplace mantel. A strange-looking angel with only half her head covered with the gilded thread. Suddenly, her tiredness disappeared. Finishing with their planned decorations would be perfect for getting her mind off Luc. Starting with the gingerbread cookies. She bustled into her room and dropped the packages on the closest surface, rummaging through for the smallest one.

She cast a wistful eye at the dresses lying about, but turned and walked down the hallway. "Ame, here's what we need for the—" At the sight of Luc standing near the table, sipping coffee, she stopped, her gaze caught by his intense one.

How could she have a normal conversation about cookies when this magnificent man was in the same room?

"Here's coffee, Carni. Oh, are those the spices?"

Carni blinked and turned, walking to where Ame held out the cup. "Thanks. I wasn't sure how much to buy." She set the package in front of Ame and sipped at the hot brew.

"Food's almost ready. Carni, do you want one egg or two?"

Her stomach jumped at the thought of sitting at the table and eating an entire meal while being ignored by Luc. "Is there bread? Maybe just some bread with jam. I can get it myself then I've got to straighten my belongings. I'm so sorry to have left my room..." Her gaze shot to Luc, to where he stood at the window. "I mean the office, a mess. If there's hot water, I'd like to take a basin to, um, there and freshen up a bit." She knew she was rambling, but someone had to fill the silence.

Before Ame could respond, Carni headed to the kitchen, grabbed what she needed and headed back to her room. She'd have to stop thinking of it as her room. An office—the room was really Luc's office. She was a guest and would be leaving. With the door closed behind her, she set her cup and plate on the top of the desk and slumped into the wooden chair.

If she let them, her feelings would overwhelm her and she'd start sobbing. And she was not a crier. She jumped up and went to the closest open valise, folding and tucking her belongings into tidy order. With all her heart, she wished she could tuck away her growing feelings for Luc in such an easy way.

****

Luc tossed down the heavy gloves and hammer and stretched his stiff fingers. No amount of nail pounding was going to release the tension running through his body. He called himself all kinds of fool for his actions the previous night.

Why hadn't he resisted her?

Why had he allowed himself a taste of Carni's sweetness? A sweetness, that now, he didn't know if he could live without.

"Hey, boss." Rey approached, leading a yearling into the corral. "There's another section on the east wall that might need patching."

Luc glared at his foreman. "And you say this because…?"

A wide smile peeking from under his moustache, Rey shrugged. "You're working with the energy of two men. Might as well get the most from your actions."

Unwilling to admit Rey was right, Luc walked away from his implements and headed toward the tack room. Always something to do in there. One step into the barn, and he inhaled the familiar scents of hay, horses and leather. Scents that calmed him.

Matro looked up from the saddle he oiled. "What you think, boss? Looks okay, no?"

Luc ran a hand over the intricate toolings that were Matro's trademark, admiring the time the old man took in making each saddle different. "A fine addition to the Bar-T tack."

"You need something, boss?"

"I'm looking for…" He hesitated, knowing he couldn't touch a thing in here without making Matro think he wasn't doing his job. "Uh, for more nails. Rey says there's another section of the barn to be repaired." His thoughts were scrambled all because he couldn't get a certain red-haired woman off his mind.

"Sí, the wall by Hades' stall. That horse likes to kick."

Luc moved toward the stall of his favorite horse and grabbed the halter from a nearby nail. His hand was on the latch when he heard his name and turned toward the open doorway.

"Mr. Luc, come quick." Ame ran toward the barn, skirts held high, hair straggling from her bun. "Oh, Mr. Luc, where are you?"

Luc dropped the halter and strode the distance, spotting Rey run up to the distraught housekeeper and grab her by the arms. His footsteps halted. He leaned a forearm on the wall just inside the barn door. Waited and watched.

As they talked, Rey lifted a hand to brush back tendrils of her blonde hair.

When had this happened? These two were obviously on friendlier terms than he'd known. Luc remembered using the same caring gesture the previous night on Carni's silky hair. He straightened. Best not dwell on last night.

Rey slid an arm around her shoulders, turning her toward the barn. They walked the remaining distance side by side.

Luc stepped through the doorway and into the sunlight. "I'm here. What's wrong?"

Ame pulled away from Rey and hurried forward. "Mr. Luc, he's taken Carni."

Carni. Just the mention of her name made his chest tighten. "Who took her?"

"Sheriff Taylor."

"What?" Dread slowed his thoughts. Carni's words about Buck scrutinizing her at the mercantile rang in his ears. And her furtive movements of snuggling close, trying to keep from being seen. Luc hadn't given her statement enough thought. He'd been more concerned with saving them from the storm.

Even her story of her past association hadn't fully registered. He'd been too focused on them being alone and the enticing treats she offered.

Ame grabbed his arm. "She's under arrest and the sheriff took her to jail." Tears welled up in her light eyes, and she wrapped her arms around her middle. "I know Carni is a little wild, always has been, but he claims she robbed stagecoaches."

No! His hands drew into fists, and he stared at Amethyst. "She didn't rob them."

"I didn't want to believe him either, but he had a wanted poster." Her shoulders slumped.

How much should he reveal about Carni's activities? Hell, the news would be all over town within the hour. He put a hand on Ame's shoulder. "I'm telling you, she was never there."

Rey stepped close, dark brows drawn low. "Are you saying you knew this about her?"

"We did some talking on the trip to town." Their other activities flashed through his thoughts, and he shook his head. "I learned about her connection to the Hegarty gang last night."

"Oh, no. It's true?" Ame gasped and covered her mouth with a shaky hand. "What will Momma and Poppa say?"

Rey drew her close, his dark gaze steady on Luc's. "What do we do, boss?"

Luc recognized his foreman's act of staking his claim on his woman and admired him for making a decision. "Not we this time, friend. Only me. I intend to talk with the sheriff." Luc turned to head back into the barn. "Matro, get Hades' saddle."

Ame followed and grabbed his forearm. "Please help my sister."

Luc paused, forcing a grim smile as he looked into Ame's concerned gaze. His thoughts already worked through the form that help could possibly take. "She won't spend the night in jail. I promise you."

Chapter Eight

Thirty minutes later, Luc and Hades galloped into Wayside Gap. No brilliant plan for helping Carni had materialized during the ride to town. He tied off Hades at the rail and jumped onto the boardwalk in front of the sheriff's office. Two strides took him to the door. He wrenched the knob, ready to tear a strip off Buck Taylor's hide.

The door didn't budge. Damn. He moved to the window to look inside, but the shades were drawn. With a snap, he pivoted and scanned both sides of the street. No sign of the heavy-set man.

Luc strode across the muddy street toward the Lucky Thistle Saloon, ignoring the mud spatters being flung by his steps. He banged on the closed door. "Matheson, you in there?" He leaned an ear against the door and heard the hollow clump of chairs being set onto a wooden floor. "Broc, it's Luc Tarrant. I'm looking for the sheriff."

A lock clicked and one side of the double doors opened. Broc leaned a shoulder against the other door, eyes squinted against the bright light. "Morning, Luc. Or is it afternoon? Now why would I have the sheriff in my establishment before the doors are even open for business?" He raked a hand through tousled black hair.

Luc glanced at his friend, noting the saloon owner's unbuttoned shirt and suspender straps hanging loose at his hips. "Right. I forgot, your day is just starting."

"Can't help you with the sheriff. Probably went home for his noon meal." He stifled a yawn. "What's the problem?"

"Need to talk to him about a prisoner."

"Prisoner, huh? No fights here last night. Nobody was hauled off because of drunkenness." Broc straightened, interest sharpening his gaze. "In fact, we closed early because of the storm. Who's the prisoner?"

Luc hated the idea of spreading rumors, but wondered if his friend might be of help. "A houseguest of mine. She's my housekeeper's sister."

"She?" Broc waited, dark eyebrow raised. "Surely, there's more."

Luc paced to the edge of the boardwalk and scanned the street, hoping to spot the sheriff on his way back to the jail. No luck. "Miss Carnelian Wendell. But this is a mistake. She's not guilty."

Broc stepped back and waved a hand toward the dark saloon. "Come inside, buddy. You look like you could use a cup of coffee. I know I definitely could."

Luc shook his head. He had to do something, anything that would help Carni. "No, I'll go looking for the sheriff. Thanks." He raised a hand in farewell and headed back across the street.

"Good luck, Luc. If a woman's involved, you're going to need it." Broc's chuckle followed him.

Luc waited while a wagon rolled past, raising his hat in greeting to the Widow McNally. Once across the street, he ducked down the alley and around to the back side of the jail. "Carni, you hear me?"

"Oh, Luc. You came."

"Of course, I did." At the desolate note in her voice, his chest tightened. "When I find the sheriff, I aim to talk sense into him."

"Luc, he has a wanted poster."

He hated not being able to see her face. "Ame told me." He spotted her small hands on the bars, but knew she'd be too short to look outside the cell. An ugly word that churned his gut.

Carni was in a dank cell, and he couldn't get to her. In a single flash, he realized that reaching her was the most important thing he could do.

"Of course, the likeness is horrible. Not flattering, at all." A high-pitched laugh sounded.

Putting on a brave front. He admired that. "I'll figure something out, Carni. I promise." He stepped to the building and rested a hand on the rough wood of the wall, somehow wishing her hand was on the other side. "I wanted you to know I'm close by."

"Luc, I hear the front door. I think the sheriff's back."

With long strides, Luc rounded the building, jumped to the boardwalk and burst through the sheriff's office door. "Buck, we need to talk about the prisoner."

Buck Taylor hung his hat on a rack of deer antlers on the wall and sauntered over to his desk. "Tarrant, you came into town. Saves me a trip back out to your ranch."

Why would the sheriff return to the Bar-T? Luc clenched his jaw before he burst out with a retort that he'd regret. No one at the ranch was involved. He had to concentrate on what he knew. "Show me the poster."

The sheriff pulled out the top desk drawer and withdrew a wrinkled piece of paper then tossed it on the desk.

Luc grabbed it and took his time reading the contents. "Miss Connie Winston (aka Dolly Watson) wanted for questioning in relation to robberies on the following occasions." He scanned the list of dates, locations, and a variety of stagecoach companies.

Then he studied the sketch. Carni was right. The likeness wasn't good.

Taking another few moments, Luc reread the physical description. The height was wrong and no mention of eye color was made. In fact, the only feature that was the same in the description was her red hair.

An idea formed, but he needed a bit more information before he moved forward. Without raising his head, he asked, "What made you bring in my houseguest?"

"Did you read the description?" The sheriff waved a beefy hand at the poster. "The part about red hair?"

"I saw it." He shrugged and tossed the sheet back on the desk. "Doesn't mean much."

"Not many women passing this way with red hair."

"Not many women passing this way at all, Buck. You got nothing here. The name's not even right. Some call her Connie, others Dolly." He leaned his hands on the desk and narrowed his gaze. "Which one of those women did you arrest?"

"Well, the lady claims her name is Carnelian Wendell." Buck let out a short laugh. "That's a made-up name if ever I heard one. Miss Ame even went along with that story."

"The woman is her sister, and Miss Ame's full name is Amethyst. Don't you think she'd know?"

He lifted a heavy shoulder and shook his head. "Family covers for family."

"I want to see her." He forced an even tone to his voice, knowing he could be pushing his luck with this know-it-all lawman.

"What do you have to say to a thief?"

Luc steamed and had to force back his anger. He'd heard Carni's story. She didn't deserve to pay for someone else's bad judgment. "You've made a mistake."

"Oh, I have?" The sheriff leaned back in his chair, the wood creaking in protest. "How's that?"

Now his idea was fully formed, and Luc had to play it out. "The woman you've got back there in your jail cell has traveled from Ft. Worth to Wayside Gap at my request. She's here for a month to see if we suit." He braced his legs apart and folded his arms over his chest, aiming for a confident stance. "She's my mail-order bride-to-be."

Buck sat forward, eyes narrowed into a squint. "Why didn't you say that first?"

"Had my reasons. Mailing away for a bride could be a tricky business. Don't know who might answer an advertisement." Luc treaded on dangerous ground here. Did he force the sheriff's hand or did he let the idea simmer? "I had to see the charges for myself. Bet you'd do the same."

Buck stood and paced to the door dividing the office from the cells. "But the red hair and the fancy clothes?"

"Of course, she'd want to make a good impression." His thoughts went to the piles of clothes decorating his office at the ranch. Or several good impressions.

"I talked with Mrs. Reinhard after the two of you left the mercantile." He slammed his hand down on the desk. "That woman put fifty dollars against your account. Explain that."

Luc stilled. At the time, he'd meant to ask her about her reasoning. Battling the storm had sent all thoughts of that transaction from his mind. "Part of her dowry. Her father owns a shipping company in Houston." Good thing he'd listened to all her chattering on their trip into town the previous day. Had that been only less than twenty-four hours earlier?

"Did you check with Einhardt? She hired a cart and that piebald horse of his for a month."

The sheriff ran a hand over his face. "Well, you do seem to know enough about the woman."

He set his features and stared. "I want to see her. Now."

Buck dug into his pocket and pulled out a ring of keys. With one last glance over his shoulder, he moved to the door and opened it. "Follow me, Tarrant."

Luc walked into the back of the sheriff's office, hoping he hadn't set himself up for disgrace in the way he'd stretched the truth.

Carni sat on the bench against the far wall, something white clutched in her hands. "Luc!" At the sight of him, she stood and crossed to the bars, grabbing hold with one hand.

The trusting look in her eyes went straight to his heart. He hadn't made a mistake. In three strides, he'd reached her and covered her hand with his. The other reached through the bars to caress her cheek.

"Step back."

With reluctance, he pulled back his hand, but held his ground. "Are you okay?"

A wan smile flashed then she nodded. "Just a little cold."

For the first time, he noticed she wore a silky green dress. No jacket or shawl, and no blanket lay across the mattress on the cot. "Where's your coat?"

"The sheriff said he had to inspect it for possible weapons." She turned a disparaging gaze on the sheriff. "Did you finish your search and is the garment still in one piece?"

The sheriff hitched up his belt. "I'll get on that, soon as you answer a couple questions. Mr. Tarrant here has been telling me a bit about your reason for being in Wayside Gap."

Carni glanced at Luc with lowered brows, her mouth drawn into a straight line.

Luc put as much encouragement into his gaze as he could muster. He told himself she was smart and would catch on to the details of his story.

"Yes? What is the question?" She squared her shoulders and looked at the sheriff.

"Tell me where you were before your trip here."

Her head angled toward him.

"Missy," Sheriff Taylor's voice was sharp. "Look at me when you answer."

Luc crossed his arms over his chest to disguise his fisted hands. God, what had he done? If she answered differently, he could be condemning her to a trial in front of the judge in San Angelo.

"In Ft. Worth, at my brother Jasper's." She leaned toward the bars. "Before that, I was in Santa Fe with my oldest brother, Malachite."

Luc let out a breath. One down. How many more?

The sheriff muttered something about names then asked, "Why'd you pay Mrs. Reinhard for Tarrant's account?"

She stiffened. "I may be a houseguest, but I pay my own way, sir. I've added myself and a rented horse to Mr. Tarrant's household. We both have to eat." She shifted her weight from foot to foot.

That's the spirit. That's the woman he loved. Luc's thoughts whirled. *Loved?* Was that the truth?

"Tell me about Luc here."

Luc closed his eyes for a moment then steeled himself to take what would come. He'd stepped over the line. Now, he'd have to watch her go down.

"About Luc?" Her hands gripped the bars tighter, and she moved her head left.

"Don't turn around."

"He's stern but fair. He cares for the people who work for him." She shivered and briskly rubbed her hands up and down her arms.

"Damn it, Taylor. Can't you see the woman is freezing?" Luc stepped back into the office, looked at the area for her coat then yanked open a closet door. A couple of blankets lay stacked on the wooden shelves. He spotted her coat bunched in a heap but thought better than riling the sheriff by bringing that along. Grabbing a blanket, he walked back to the space in front of the cells and extended it through the bars. He stared down the sheriff, daring him to say anything against his actions.

The sheriff shrugged. "Take the blanket."

She moved to where Luc stood and reached out a hand. "Thanks."

What he wanted was to pull her to the bars and whisper reassurances that everything would be all right. Somehow, he figured the sheriff wouldn't go for that plan.

"Now tell me what Luc means to you."

Carni arranged the blanket over her shoulders before answering. "Don't you think you're getting personal here, sheriff?"

The sheriff's gaze narrowed. "Are you refusing to answer?"

With dread churning in his gut, Luc leaned back against the wall. Her dander was up and now she was going to let fly with the first thing that sprang to mind.

Chapter Nine

"I'm not refusing, I'm confused. What do my feelings for Luc have to do with the fact I'm locked in here?" She spread her hands to indicate the cell, thoughts racing at the direction of the sheriff's questions.

Why had his questions turned personal? What had Luc told him?

"You've been in Wayside Gap less than four days." The sheriff shifted and leaned an elbow against the bars. "Are you saying you've formed an attachment to Mr. Tarrant?"

Her heart jerked and her pulse raced. Attachment? Why would the sheriff use that word? If she could just see Luc's eyes, she'd know how to answer. "These questions are beginning to sound a little like a trial."

"Familiar with the format for a trial, are you?" His lips turned down in a jeer. "Yours, perhaps?"

How dare he! "Of course not." She flipped a strand of hair over her shoulder and jutted out her chin, pinning him with a cold look.

Luc cleared his throat. "We're wasting time here. Sheriff, just ask her the question."

What question? Luc's words sounded tense. What did that mean? Oh, how she wished she could see his face.

"No, I have another plan." The key rattled in the heavy lock.

As it swung open, Carni stared at the iron door, her breath catching in her throat. What did the sheriff's action mean? She couldn't afford to show any of the runaway indecision she felt. Grabbing the sides of the blanket, she squared her shoulders and walked past the smirking lawman.

Luc stood by the doorway to the outer office, arms spread. "Hello, darlin'."

Darlin'? She hesitated. An endearment from Luc? He hadn't used them before. No matter. She was out of that horrible cell. Taking only a moment to gaze at his handsome face, she rushed to him and wrapped her arms around his waist. "Thank you for—"

Luc's mouth devoured her words and nibbled at her lips, his embrace pressing her tight against his body.

After his indifferent attitude of this morning, she held back for only a second then melted into the kiss. Relief at being out of the cell was nothing compared to the relief that Luc's feelings for her hadn't disappeared. She stretched on tiptoes to press her mouth more fully against his, savoring the prickle of his beard.

Her Luc had come to her rescue.

The hollow scuffle of boots on wooden planks sounded. "Okay, folks. I see that you care for one another."

At the sheriff's words, Carni was brought back to the reality of their location.

"Like I told you, sheriff." Luc's hold loosened and he cupped the back of her head with his hand, trailing kisses against her hair, close to her ear. "Trust me."

His whisper was fervent. Why? She tucked her head against Luc's chest and listened to his thumping heart. Like she had the previous night, when their bodies had done all the talking, their actions displaying the desire they felt for one another.

If she could trust her body to this man, she could trust wherever his words took them.

Luc dropped one arm and snuggled her close to his side. "Now, can we head back to the ranch? I got chores waiting."

"Nope." Buck Taylor shook his head and hooked his thumbs in his waistband.

Her gaze sought Luc's, but he stared at the sheriff, a muscle in his jaw jerking.

"You'll be heading to the church."

What? Carni gasped and her head whipped around. "The church? Whatever for?"

Luc's hand gripped her shoulder, and his boot pushed against her shoe. "I'm listening."

"Well, you say this lady came to your ranch as a mail-order bride..." The sheriff rocked back on his boot heels, a grin twitching at the corners of his mouth.

Carni swallowed hard and fought to keep her surprise from showing. Mail-order bride? Did she look like—? Was that what Luc told the sheriff? She could barely believe what she was hearing.

"And since you obviously have..." He cleared his throat and glanced to the side. "...affection toward each other..." His grin grew as he jangled the key ring in his hand.

"I apologize for that public display, Sheriff Taylor." Luc shrugged. "I've been worried."

Oh, butter wouldn't melt in Luc's mouth at that moment. What had happened to change his attitude?

The sheriff waved a hand, indicating they should move into the office. "Seems like a good day for a wedding."

For just a moment, Carni sagged against Luc in relief. Then the full meaning of the sheriff's words hit. Wedding? As in to love and honor until death do us part. She couldn't let Luc follow through with this charade.

With his hands cupping her shoulders, Luc turned her and looked straight into her eyes. "I agree, Sheriff. And any bride of mine will be dressed better than this for such an event." With two fingers, he plucked off the blanket and let it fall to the wooden flooring. He stepped into the closet and picked up her coat, draping it over her shoulders, and then held out his elbow. "Shall we, Carni?"

They walked out to the boardwalk. He turned toward the uphill side of town.

Had he really just said 'bride'? She pressed against his side and whispered just loud enough for him to hear, "Luc, what are you doing?"

"Hush, Carni." Luc laid his hand over hers and patted.

"You don't have to call the sheriff's bluff."

He shot her a sideways glance, brows drawn low. "Do you want back inside that jail cell?"

She cringed and shuddered. "Well, no."

"Then I'm saving your behind."

"Hey, Luc. I see you found the sheriff and the mysterious prisoner."

Carni glanced across the street toward the Lucky Thistle Saloon and spotted a tall, dark-haired man waving.

"That I did, Broc."

Mr. Reinhard swept the boards in front of the mercantile and nodded as they passed. "What's going on, Sheriff?"

"Escorting these folks to a wedding."

"A wedding? Trude, come look at this."

Carni felt heat rising in her cheeks. Oh Lordy, what was happening? She didn't dare turn around. What if the sheriff had grabbed a shotgun from the jail?

Maybe that's why Luc had agreed.

From behind, she heard the stamp of horses' hooves and the rattle of wagon wheels. What now?

"Oh, thank heavens, Mr. Luc. You got her

out of jail."

Amethyst. Carni closed her eyes and stumbled.

Luc stopped and turned toward the street, his arm clamping her tight to his body. "Thought I told you two to stay on the ranch."

"Sorry, boss." Rey slowed the horses. "I had to drive or she would have ridden on horseback. And we both know what happened the last time she tried."

"What?" Carni leaned forward to see her sister. The relief in Ame's shiny eyes brought a scratchiness to her own. Ame had been worried. More worried than normal.

"Keep walking, folks." The sheriff's voice boomed.

Hurrying footsteps clunked from behind. "Did you hear? There's gonna be a wedding."

Carni recognized the voice of the storekeeper's wife. As much as she liked being the center of attention, even she had to admit, this was turning into a spectacle.

"Carnelian, is this true? You and Mr. Luc?"

Oh, Lord, would her sister be the undoing of Luc's arranged story? She leaned forward to make eye contact with Ame who sat perched on the edge of the cart seat as it kept pace. "Yes, isn't the sheriff so smart? Luc and I couldn't hide our true feelings. This mail-order bride deal has been a success." She gave her sister an exaggerated wink and tried to fill her expression with pleading. For once in your life, play along,

Ame. Don't be a stickler for the truth.

With a frown marring her brow, Ame hesitated.

Carni nudged an elbow into Luc's side, needing him to back her up.

He jerked then glanced at her, eyes widening. "Oh, yeah. Good timing, Rey. You and Ame can be our witnesses."

"Oh, sure boss. I'll let the preacher know." Rey snapped the reins and hastened the horse toward the white church on the hill.

In a few places, patches of snow clung to the shaded spots of ground. As each step took her closer to a change she wouldn't be able to undo, Carni's thoughts sorted through the unreality for what she knew to be true.

Today was Christmas Eve.

She was walking toward a marriage to a man who ranched in the middle of the west Texas prairie.

This grouping of no more than a dozen buildings comprised the biggest population center for more than fifty miles.

Echoes of many footsteps on wooden planks resounded behind them. How many people followed? She peeked over her right shoulder and looked square into the chest of a very determined sheriff.

"Second thoughts, Miss?" His sneer showed a row of uneven teeth.

"No, sir." She whipped around her head and faced the boardwalk leading to the church.

Luc covered her hand with his and squeezed.

His strength seemed to seep into her body. But her stomach tickled with butterflies dancing, and she pressed a hand to her waist. She felt the cloth angel in her pocket—the one she'd been decorating for the fireplace mantel.

Luc leaned over and whispered, "There's a patch of bare ground coming up before we climb to the church. Shall we break and run?"

The fact he tried to lighten the moment warmed her. "Sorry, not a fast runner."

His grip tightened as they descended the last set of stairs and stepped onto the hard-packed dirt. The rest of the walk went by in a blur. Next thing she knew, she stood in the front of the church, facing Luc with a scraggly bunch of dried flowers that had been thrust into her hands at the last minute.

People still eased into pews and whispered among themselves. Obviously, spontaneous weddings didn't happen often—at least not on Thursday afternoons, the day before Christmas.

A side door opened and the preacher hurried in, still buttoning his collar. He hesitated when he looked at the numerous visitors in the audience and then approached the couple. "Good afternoon, folks."

She nodded at the kindly older gentleman, uncertainty stealing her words.

"Preacher Evans," Luc's voice rumbled.

"Your foreman shared the circumstances of

this event." His lips drew into a frown. "I must hear your assurances that you both come to this union of your own free will."

Luc's amber gaze caressed her face, touching on her lips and returned to her eyes. "I'm here because I want to be."

Was that the truth she saw in his eyes or just the words he knew he had to say? "Me, too."

"Folks, quiet please." Preacher Evans raised both hands and slowly lowered them. "Seems word has spread about the wedding today, and I always welcome people into the house of the Lord. I request silence to honor the spiritual joining of a loving man and woman into the holy state of matrimony."

As the preacher spoke, Carni heard only phrases, "sacred and inward union...Church does bless...loving purpose...abiding will."

Then the preacher instructed them to face each other and repeat words that he spoke. Carni looked into Luc's gaze, hazel eyes full of warmth and love, and she uttered words of having and holding, for richer and poorer, until death parted them, and pledging her faith.

"Due to the unusual circumstances, I doubt a ring is present. But we'll continue as if there were one."

Carni looked at Luc and shrugged.

Luc's gaze landed on the cloth angel in her hand, and he touched the golden threads on the angel's head. "This will work for now. I promise to replace it with a real one."

His tone was so sincere, Carni dared to believe Luc meant what he said.

With a pocketknife, he cut one of the threads and tied it onto the third finger of her left hand as the preacher intoned the proper words. Luc raised her hand to his mouth and kissed the shiny thread. "I do."

Tears burned the back of her eyes and her hands shook. She couldn't believe Luc would speak untruths in front of the people he expected to grow old with and the community's preacher. As he'd spoken the words, his gaze hadn't wavered.

Could she hope this was more than a ruse to get her out of jail?

Her turn. She bit her lip and listened to what the preacher said, worrying she'd never live up to those sentiments. One look into Luc's loving gaze, and she knew he represented all she'd ever wanted. Peacefulness enveloped her heart. "Yes, I do."

Luc leaned down and brushed a sweet kiss on her lips and whispered, "I've found my holiday angel."

Carnelian Wendell Tarrant blinked hard to stem threatening tears. "And I've found a home. In your arms."